His nod was barely perceptible.

As desperately as Sara wanted to look away from the hurt on his face, she couldn't. His eyes glistened and he blinked. Bending down, he picked up his jacket. She hadn't seen it on the floor behind the coffee table. At the sight of the scarred brown leather, her pulse skipped. She tried not to remember the scent of it but couldn't block it out.

He stood up, slid his arms into the jacket. He hadn't said a word after her reply. Sara rose to her feet but couldn't have moved away from that spot if she'd wanted to. Her legs felt nailed to the floor. Reece had told the truth—this was not the same man who walked out on her. His body had filled out, and his face had lost its boyish look. A long-sleeved black T-shirt fit tight across well-defined muscles. She wondered how he could move his arms in the snug jacket. The sky blue eyes she saw in her dreams seemed deeper set and held the look of a man who had lived hard for the past two years.

As he zipped his jacket, he looked at her with a slight smile that hinted of regret. "I'll be at Mom and Dad's until the day after Christmas if. . ." Leaving the sentence unfinished, he walked past her then turned and reached out to her. The back of his hand touched her cheek. His eyes gleamed with tears. "Sara. . ." His voice was soft and hoarse, just above a whisper. "I still love you."

He took his gloves from the shelf and walked out the door.

A Wisconsin resident, **BECKY MELBY** has four sons and nine grandchildren. When not writing or spending time with family, Becky enjoys motorcycle rides with her husband and reading. Becky has coauthored several books with her writing partner Cathy Wienke for Barbour Publishing.

Wisconsin native **CATHY WIENKE** and her husband have two sons, a daughter, and two grandchildren. Her favorite pastimes include reading and walking her dog. Cathy has coauthored numerous books with her writing partner Becky Melby for Barbour Publishing.

Visit their Web site at www.melby-wienke.com

Books by Becky Melby and Cathy Wienke

HEARTSONG PRESENTS
HP98—Beauty for Ashes
HP169—Garment of Praise
HP242—Far Above Rubies
HP822—Walk with Me
HP837—Dream Chasers

Don't miss out on any of our super romances. Write to us at the following address for information on our newest releases and club information.

Heartsong Presents Readers' Service
PO Box 721
Uhrichsville, OH 44683

Or visit www.heartsongpresents.com

Stillwater Promise

Becky Melby and Cathy Wienke

Heartsong Presents

To Becky Melby, Patti Haas, Nancy Johnson, and Diane Ross—I am so blessed having been graced with your friendships that are filled with love, laughter, and prayers.

Thank you! Cathy

To my father-in-law, Irvin Curtis Melby—the real storyteller in the family. Thank you for entertaining three generations of Melbys and for painting such vivid pictures of life in God's country. And in loving remembrance of Lillian Irene Melby, the woman who raised the man of integrity I fell in love with and taught me that love grows like a tree adding branches. . .there will always be enough to go around.

Love, Becky

A special thank-you to JoAnne, our fabulous editor (and her assistant, Jodi), and to Margie for her great eye. Thank you Bill, Cynthia, Jan, Tiffany, Carrie, and the amazing Pearl Girls—Patti, Eileen, and Lee—for awesome editing, ideas, and prayer support. And to Sara's husband, Brian, for Korgy.

A note from the Author:
We love to hear from our readers! You may correspond with us by writing:

Becky Melby and Cathy Wienke
Author Relations
PO Box 721
Uhrichsville, OH 44683

ISBN 978-1-60260-518-3

STILLWATER PROMISE

Our mission is to publish and distribute inspirational products offering exceptional value and biblical encouragement to the masses.

PRINTED IN THE U.S.A.

one

"Not every princess has a prince."

Sara Lewis laughed at the obstinate looks on her daughters' faces.

"Uh-huh. They do so." Zoe, her four-year-old, narrowed her eyes. Deep furrows creased her forehead, and her lips pressed together in a tight line. Snuggled next to her under the faded pink bedspread, two-year-old Sadie mimicked the expression.

Sara tweaked two miniature noses. "Let me tell my story."

"Will the prince be at the end?"

No, the prince will be at the beginning. And then he will fly away to England, leaving the princess all alone but not in a castle. "I promise the story will have a happy ending, okay?"

Zoe folded her arms across Mister Peabody—her worn, stained, once-pink stuffed dog. Sadie folded her arms across her purple pajamas. "Okay."

"Once upon a time, Lady Sara—"

"That's you!"

"Well, it's make-believe me."

Pale blond curls bounced. "Is make-believe Zoe and make-believe Sadie in the story?"

"Absolutely."

Sara stared into two pairs of sky blue eyes. Her girls had her hair but not her green eyes. Those sky blue eyes were too much like their father's. She swallowed, smiled, and began the story for the third time.

"Lady Sara and her two little princesses left their tiny little apartment in Pine Bluff and went out for a walk in the woods to pick wildflowers. They were so busy picking pink roses and purple violets and white daisies that they didn't realize how deep in the woods they had wandered."

Zoe's eyes widened. "They were lost, huh?"

"Well, they thought they were. But just then, Princess Sadie found a shiny diamond on the ground, and then, just a few steps away, Princess Zoe found another one and another one. The diamonds were leading them down a path, deeper into the woods."

"And they got loster!"

"Shh. Just listen." Sara tapped the tip of her finger to her lips. "All of a sudden, the path turned and there in front of them was a ginormous castle! All white and sparkly, with a green roof and green shutters and a great big porch with a swing and lots and lots of shiny white rocking chairs."

"Like that one!" Zoe pointed to the mural on the wall. "Is the castle far, far away? Is it in Myoming like Nana and Papa?"

"Is it by Babe?" Sadie sat straight up, white blond wisps waving as she moved.

"It's pretty far from Babe the Blue Ox. The castle is in Stillwater, and that's *still* in Minnesota. It's about as far away as the Disney Store."

"The one at Mall of 'Merica?"

"Yup."

Sadie held up one finger, her sign for the world to stop and give her center stage. "We goed there with Grandma Connie one time."

Sara rubbed the muscle at the back of her neck that tightened reflexively at the mention of her mother-in-law. In just under twelve hours, Connie Lewis would descend upon her girls like an overcaffeinated toucan and whisk them away for three days while Sara went to work. After Sunday it would take Sara four days to get them back to some semblance of a calm routine, and then the circus would began all over again. "We *went* there with Grandma Connie," she corrected.

"Uh-huh. To Yego Yand."

Zoe gave an exasperated sigh. "Say L–L–Lego, Sadie."

"L–L–Yego."

Sara held up one finger. "It's almost time to turn out the light. Should I tell the story another time?"

"No. We'll be quiet." Zoe patted the pillow next to her. "Lie down, Sadie, and shut your eyes and 'magine the castle."

Sara stifled a yawn, thinking she'd give about anything to just lie down, close her eyes, and imagine her Stillwater castle.

❧

Still sitting on the edge of the bed long after her girls had fallen asleep, Sara stared at her daughters in their hand-me-down pajamas. Outside, ice-laced snow pelted the window, gathering along the ledge. The wind whistled around the corner of the old building. Sara wrapped her sweatshirt jacket a little tighter but shivered anyway.

This was her last year of secondhand living. By this time next winter, she'd have a fireplace to curl up next to after tucking Zoe and Sadie into their canopy bed. By this time next year, she'd be decorating the Stillwater Inn for Christmas.

She pulled the shade down and began her nightly ritual. Books in the book basket, sorted by size. Plastic toys in the plastic bin, stuffed animals in the net that hung in the corner of the room. She straightened a picture, turned off the lamp, and picked up a dirty sock and a pair of 3T jeans on her way out the door.

Three bowls sat on the small, scarred table pushed against the wall between her kitchenette and living room. Remnants of Hamburger Helper, sans hamburger, covered the bottoms of the bowls. She cleared the table and wiped it off then took off her red-striped apron and moved a large cardboard box from the counter to the table. In it were ten white paper bags with snowman faces made from felt and yarn. Each bag was filled with Christmas cookies. She glanced at the clock on the stove. All she had yet to do was make the tags. From index cards she'd picked up at the dollar store, she cut five freehand snowflakes and printed names on each. She'd just finished attaching the tag labeled "Raquel & Allison" when there was a knock on the door. As usual, Mattie Jennet was on time.

Sara opened the door to find Mattie, in her heavy EMT jacket, shaking off snow like a wet puppy. "It's miserable out there. Two accidents since four o'clock."

"You could have waited until tomorrow."

Running fingers through her dark blond hair streaked with silver, Mattie smiled. "Neither sleet nor snow nor a daughter in labor will keep a Sanctuary mentor from her appointed rounds."

"What?" Sara held the door for Mattie. "Shouldn't you be with Sydney?"

"Nah. That's what husbands are for. I've delivered my share of babies, but I'd be a wreck with my own daughter." Mattie unzipped her jacket and pointed to a cell phone and a pager clipped to her belt. "So I'm on rescue squad *and* grandbaby call tonight. Are the girls asleep?"

Sara nodded. "They were exhausted after helping me bake cookies all day." She pointed to the box on the table. "Would you mind taking cookies to the Middletons and Gwyneth and the new residents?"

"No problem. That's so sweet of you."

"Hey, you paid for the ingredients."

"No." Mattie's voice held an undercurrent of maternal sternness. "We give you vouchers, but you make choices. You could have spent that money on candy bars or magazines."

Embarrassed yet quietly warmed by the compliment, Sara stuck her hands in her pockets.

Mattie slipped off her boots, laid her jacket on the floor, and walked over to the box. "Do you have any idea how easy you make my job?"

Sara shrugged.

"Out of the twelve apartments in the Sanctuary program, yours is the only one I can walk into without taking a deep breath and praying for patience. . .and certainly the only one where the floors are clean enough to eat off and the soup cans are alphabetized!" Mattie pulled out a chair and sat at the kitchen table. "I've decided to create a new award. I'm calling it the Bounce Award. And you're the first recipient."

Sara let her look of confusion suffice for an answer.

"You bounce back faster and better than anyone I've ever met. Your husband walks out on you, and you bounce. You're smoked out of your apartment, and you bounce. A twister destroys your trailer. . .and you bounce back to us, still smiling and being a mom to everyone in this building. You're amazing."

"Amazing will be when I bounce out of here and your church is no longer subsidizing my food and rent." Sara wrapped her arms around her middle. "How about some tea?"

"That would be wonderful, but you're not going to get me off track that easily. You need to learn to take a compliment, young lady."

Opening the lid on the teapot and holding it under the faucet, Sara repeated the shrug. "It's. . .uncomfortable."

"You'll have to get used to it when your bed-and-breakfast starts getting rave reviews."

Sara laughed. "Only three hundred and forty-seven days until the Stillwater Inn is under the management of Sara Lewis. I'm planning a grand reopening." She took two cups from the cupboard and brought them to the table. After shoving the cardboard box toward the wall, she sat down. "Let's get the accountability questions out of the way in case you have to run to the hospital." She took an exaggerated breath. "I haven't smoked, gotten drunk, used illegal substances, been with a man, or broken the law in the past seven days. I have paid my bills, stuck to my budget, gotten to work on time, kept my apartment clean, disciplined my children. . .most of the time. . .and tried to be an asset to the community. And the spiritual stuff isn't mandatory, so I'm all good."

"Like I said, you make my job easy."

"I may take over your job someday."

Leaning forward, Mattie rested her hand on Sara's. "As soon as you figure out the spiritual stuff *is* mandatory, I'll create a position in the Sanctuary program just for you."

Sara shifted in her chair, wishing the teapot would whistle. This was the part of Mattie's visits she hated. She had no doubt that Mattie Jennet was the kind of person she was because of her religious beliefs. It worked for the Jennets and most of the people Sara had met from Pineview Community Church. But it didn't work for her.

Mattie patted Sara's hand. "Do you want to know what I pray for you?"

"I. . .guess."

"I'm praying that God won't leave you alone until you admit you need Him."

The sound of pressure building in the teapot brought Sara to her feet. What would an answer to Mattie's prayer look like? A pay raise? A new husband? Or another natural disaster?

"A letter came to the church for you." Mattie ripped open a tea bag packet.

"If it's a bill, you can keep it." After the tornado, before she'd known she'd end up back in a Sanctuary apartment for the second time in two years, Sara had arranged for her mail to be forwarded to Mattie's church. Some of it still ended up there. "Is it my Visa bill?" Mattie knew every detail of her finances. Her credit card bill, much of it racked up by the man who was still legally her husband, the man she hadn't laid eyes on since Sadie was eight months old, was the final hurdle she'd have to jump before realizing her goal.

A pensive look creased the lines around Mattie's mouth. "It's not a bill. It's a letter." Slowly she reached toward her back pocket, pulled out the envelope, and laid it on the table. "It's from London. . .from James."

≈

"He thinks that's going to make everything all better? Just like that—*poof!*—five years of being a self-centered, immature, irresponsible lousy excuse for a man is just wiped away?" Sara's laugh teetered on the edge of hysteria. She kicked a stuffed pony, sending it flying at a fake green ficus tree. Mattie had left hours ago, so she ranted at the cracked living room walls.

The words of the letter were branded on her brain, burning and blistering, and no amount of raging at the walls was going to douse the pain. For the third time, she picked up the cell phone she shared with her neighbor because they were both clinging to every dollar they earned. For the third time, she slammed it back on the counter. If James were paying the bill, she'd make an overseas call in a heartbeat. But James hadn't paid a bill since Sadie was born.

Dear Sara,
  I can't possibly do justice to an apology in a letter, so consider this just my first step in the right direction.

Sara stared at the spotted beige carpeting. *No, James, your first step in the right direction was out the door.* Not that she had seen it that way at the time, of course.

There were cookie crumbs on the carpet—cookie crumbs and red and green sugar and little chocolate jimmies. She walked into her bedroom, opened the closet, and took out the carpet sweeper.

  I'm not the same man I was two years ago. I've given my life to Jesus Christ, and now I know that only God can save our marriage.

Cookie crumbs ticked against metal as the roller brush whisked them into the sweeper. *Why didn't God save our marriage back when I still loved you? Back when I begged you not to leave us? Back when Zoe sobbed herself to sleep every night, crying for her daddy?*

I'm sending you a book that a friend recommended. It's called Recipe for a Godly Wife.

Recipe? How about this for a recipe, James: one part commitment, two parts sacrifice, and a pinch of putting your dreams on hold for your kids? The carpet sweeper banged the leg of the couch, leaving a dent.

In the meantime, here are some tracts that explain the basics of what it means to be a Christian.

I know what it means to be a Christian, James. I've seen it up close in the people who gave me a place to live when you didn't, in the Sanctuary volunteers who aren't afraid to get close to recovering addicts and ex-cons and kids with AIDS.

Walking into the kitchen, she opened the cupboard under the sink and retrieved the tracts she'd shoved into the trash can. On one, fierce orange flames licked at the title—"Where Will You Spend Eternity?"

Mechanically she closed the cupboard door and stood next to the counter, tearing the tracts into minuscule pieces. Scooping the confetti into her hand, she turned and walked to the door. In worn-thin slippers she padded into the hallway and opened the front door.

Sleet stung her face as she stepped onto the porch, leaned over the railing, and opened her fist, scattering bits and pieces of angry flames into the wind.

two

"Grandma Connie's here!" Zoe flew into Sara's room in nothing but her Dora the Explorer underwear. "She has gernola."

"*Gran*ola." Sara caught Zoe and shoved an undershirt over her head. "Of course she does," she muttered. Her mother-in-law couldn't just feed the girls her homemade nuts and twigs at her house; she had to show up fifteen minutes early with her labeled zippered bags and plop them on the counter next to Sara's off-brand graham crackers and skim milk.

Sadie's squeal of delight sounded from the living room. That tone meant only one thing—Grandma Connie had brought something, probably something pink. Sara ran a brush through her hair and squared her shoulders. After practicing her smile in the mirror, she turned off the light. In her cheeriest voice she sang out, "Good morning!" as she walked into the living room.

"*Bom dia!*" Connie held Sadie by the armpits, swinging her around in a waltz pattern. "I'm practicing my Portuguese for our trip to Brazil." As they danced, something that looked like a neon rainbow bounced in Sadie's hands.

Smile glued firmly in place, Sara nodded at the plump woman in the crinkly all-cotton periwinkle blue jumper and fur-lined leather boots. Connie had been planning a trip to somewhere as long as Sara had known her, but the money in the vacation envelope always got diverted. One year it went to bee-keeping equipment, another to a spinning wheel. The last Sara knew, both were gathering dust in her in-laws' private museum, otherwise known as their garage. "What did Grandma Connie bring you, Sadie?"

13

Connie stopped spinning. The clusters of hand-sculpted red cubes that dangled from her ears didn't. She set Sadie down. "Show Mommy what the poor people in India made."

"A Christmas dress! One for Zoe, too." Sadie held out a limp, crumpled sack dress.

Sara's smile tightened. "Ah. Purple and pink and yellow and orange. . .what Christmassy colors. Say "thank you," and go get the clothes I laid out, girls."

"Wait, Sadie! Wait, Zoe!" Wooden bracelets collided on Connie's pale, pudgy arm as she waved them back. She turned to Sara. "I just read on earthgrandma.com that you should never lump your children together by saying 'kids' or 'boys' or 'girls' but should always use their names. It gives them a stronger sense of personal identity."

"Fascinating." *And what do matching rainbow dresses do to their 'personal identity'?*

"Oh, and you shouldn't always refer to them in their birth order. You don't want to establish a hierarchy in the family." She smiled at the girls. "Sadie, Zoe. . .I have an idea! Let's find the reindeer shirts I made you and get our pictures taken with Santa after we go to Grandma's t'ai chi chih class!"

"Um. . .wait." Sara's tinny laugh accompanied the finger she held in the air. "I think the shirts are dirty." The oversized sponge-painted shirts had, in fact, been worn just yesterday and were now folded next to the princess dresses and clown costumes. She didn't want Connie to know that her masterpieces had found a home in the dress-up box.

Her mother-in-law donned a quizzical look. "Dirty? How I wish you knew the meaning of the word. A little disarray would be so good for their souls, Sara."

"The sweaters I laid out will be just fine for a picture." Sara tried in vain to relax her neck muscles as she told the girls, for the second time, to go get their clothes then turned to Connie. "I thought you said they didn't have child care at your exercise class."

Connie laughed. "The boy who works at the front desk downstairs watches Sadie and Zoe for me."

Sara opened her mouth, but Connie flashed a smile like a little girl with a secret. "I had a wonderful conversation with the dean of admissions at the community college in Coon Rapids. I know his wife through the arts council, you know." She talked in a conspiratorial whisper. "And. . .he said. . .that just for me he'd guarantee that you can still get in for the spring semester! They have openings in the social work degree program, and you could take classes Monday through Thursday and still be able to keep your job."

Sara's fingernails pressed into the palms of her hands. "Thank you for checking on it." *Again.* "It's just not possible right now." *And it never will be because I DON'T WANT TO BE A SOCIAL WORKER!* Yelling in her head brought a smidgen of relief.

"Nonsense. If you had a degree, you could get paid for doing what you do anyway." Connie's hand swept toward the front door. "And you wouldn't have to live in a place like this to do it. With your low-income status, you'd qualify for a gazillion grants and loans. And"—her expression morphed into an unconvincingly sympathetic smile—"when the divorce is finalized, I'm sure you'd get even more."

The moon-shaped grooves in Sara's hands throbbed. "We haven't filed yet."

"Well yes, but when you do. . .how many times have Neil and I told you that we'd watch Zoe and Sadie? You know, if the gir—Sadie and Zoe were with us, it'd be a party every minute."

A party every minute. That was the philosophy that had turned James and his brother Brock into people who looked like adults on the outside but handled disappointment and responsibility like toddlers. When a wife and children disrupted James's dreams, he ran. When losing two friends— one to leukemia and one in a car accident—set Brock's world on end, he partied to avoid thinking and grieving.

"If I went to school for anything, it would be to finish my interior design degree."

"You'd end up decorating houses for snobby people in the Twin Cities and lose your passion for people and art. Take it from someone who tried. When I had my sculptures on display in that upscale gallery, I started thinking in dollar signs just like those people."

But your two-headed giraffes and elephants with wings didn't sell! "Interior design isn't quite the sa—"

"Art should be free. . .like air." Connie's fluffy black hair bobbed as her head shook.

Sara's tongue was sore from holding it in place with her teeth. "That's not the advice you gave James."

"Well. . ." Connie spun a wooden bracelet with a thick finger. "Music is a different story. And James is a different subject altogether." She looked up but not at Sara. Her eyes took on a glazed, faraway look. "My boy was destined to do great things."

❧

"Hey, Lewis! Quit yer lollygaggin', and give me a hand with this amp."

James set down the pen that he'd been holding an inch above the paper for the past ten minutes and waited while a Metropolitan Police car sped past the window, siren wailing, blue lights flashing. Nights in this part of London were never quiet. Over the repetitive clunking of wooden chairs being upended on tables and the bartenders' after-hours chatter, James yelled to the drummer. "Be there in a sec." He folded the unfinished letter and stuck it in the pocket of the battered leather jacket he'd bought eight years ago.

Had the first letter reached her? Maybe he'd never know. It wasn't likely she'd answer—his wife had every reason to hate him.

But something was prodding him to try. No, not something . . .Someone. The first cracks in his denial had started in July.

His best friend's nagging played a part. And the pictures his mother sent of his daughters—pictures intended to draw him home—not to his wife but to his girls—were wearing him down, too. His girls were getting so big. . .and looking so much like their mother. The conviction had been growing for months, but it had only been in the last few weeks that he'd felt the go-ahead to actually contact Sara. He'd plied his mother for details, but she was being tight-lipped about Sara's whereabouts. Her reluctance didn't surprise him—she'd never approved of Sara. He'd just about killed his mother by marrying a waitress. James was sure his little brother had the answers to all his questions, but Brock was silent for totally different reasons. Brock was protecting Sara. . .from James.

Where was she living since the tornado? What was she doing? For all he knew, she'd found someone to take his place—someone who fit the mold better than he'd been willing to.

Was he crazy to wish for another chance when Sara regretted giving him the first. . .and second?

It wasn't like he hadn't warned her. Five minutes after meeting Sara Martin, the chatty little blond behind the counter at Perk Place, he'd told her flat out that he and his band were on their way to Canada—which was just a stepping-stone to their dream goal—England. He'd warned her that she'd better turn those gorgeous green eyes on some other guy. She'd acted shocked at his comment, but James had her figured. The half can of whipping cream she'd mounded on his pumpkin pie told him all he needed to know. His buddy Reece, sitting right next to him, had gotten a dollop the size of a quarter.

If only she'd listened to him. If only he'd listened to himself.

No, Lord, I don't mean that. If she hadn't snared him with those startlingly green eyes, he wouldn't have those rumpled pictures in his wallet. And if it weren't for those two pairs of blue eyes staring up from the pictures, maybe he wouldn't have taken Reece seriously when he'd popped back in his life acting like a Jesus freak.

And if it weren't for Jesus, he was pretty sure he wouldn't have just applied for a job in Minnesota.

❧

Sara scraped the frost off her windshield with a cracked CD case as she watched the back end of Connie's Ford Escape turn the corner with Zoe and Sadie tucked in their car seats in the back. Something in her wanted to run after them, to pull the girls out of the car and hold them close for just another minute before being away from them for three days. She hadn't had a chance to ask details about the boy who watched her girls at the health club. She tried to tell herself that their grandmother wouldn't do anything to put them at risk, but it still didn't sit right with her. Unfortunately she wasn't in a position to call the shots. A stray tear hit the glass and froze as it rolled down the sloped window.

"Sara, wait up!" Allison Johansen, seventeen years old and six months pregnant by a boy who had fled the scene, waved from the porch and started down the steps, her jacket and long dishwater blond hair flapping in the wind. "Can I hitch a ride to town with you?"

"Sure. Be careful on those steps, Al."

Allison was laughing when she reached the car. "Man, I'm sick of feeling like a cow." She pointed toward the corner. "Hey, I almost asked Crazy Connie for a ride just to see the look on her face."

Sara bit down on her tongue. She was the grownup in this conversation. Besides, anything she said to Allison would find its way to her brother-in-law. Who knew which recycled words Brock might use as ammunition against Connie in a mother-son fight? "She would have given you a ride."

"Yeah, right. It drives her wacky that Brock and me hang out. You shoulda heard her hulk out on him last week."

They got in the car, and Sara turned off the country music

station. "Where am I taking you?"

"My friend Diana's house. We're just chillaxin."

"Translate, kid."

"Chillin' and relaxin'. You know, watching movies, talkin' about how lame Christmas is, and eating cookie dough all day. Just don't be a squealer, okay?"

"You really need to take your doctor's orders seriously. You don't want to end up with an emergency C-section like your mom had."

Allison blew her bangs out of her eyes. "Things have changed since back then. They have drugs for gestational diabetes now. Hey, did you know that your ex is a Bible thumper? Brock got a letter with a bunch of weird stuff in it." She widened her eyes and held her hands, fingers bent and wiggling, next to her face. "Where will yooooou spend eternity?" A wicked laugh followed.

"What does Brock think about it?"

"He thought it was funny, but. . .I don't know. He used to be into that stuff before that girl died."

"Caitlyn."

"Yeah. Hey, at least he's not into all that chanting stuff Crazy Connie does."

"Chanting? What do you mean?"

Allison shrugged. "Brock says she lights candles all over and sits on the floor in the living room, mooing like a baby cow."

Sara laughed, but the vision of Connie mooing triggered a flash of anxiety. What kind of nonsense was Connie exposing the girls to? "I think she's just doing her tai chi exercises."

"Yeah, maybe. Or maybe she's doing voodoo on you and me cuz we messed with her boys."

Nerve endings prickled along Sara's spine. Allison's perception of Connie's territorial nature surprised her. "Connie may be"—nothing positive came to mind for several seconds— "eccentric, but her heart is really in the right place."

A laugh, almost as evil sounding as the last one, came from

Allison. "Who you kidding? I hear her talking to you. She's frontin' you with all that nicey-nice, girl."

"What do you mean?"

Allison's hands folded over her belly. "I mean she's scammin' to take your kids away."

three

Working at Tippet House wasn't just a job; it was an apprenticeship. Today it was also an escape—from thoughts of James's letter and Allison's chilling words. Eight hours ago, as she'd driven up the drive lined with ice-crusted trees to the old Victorian covered in traditional "painted lady" nursery-room colors, Sara had left most of her roller-coaster emotions behind. In spite of only four hours of sleep, she was on task, ready to tackle three days of work, ready to pepper Bessie with questions and collect answers and instructions like a human DVR. Until Sunday night when she drove back down the winding lane, she'd do her best to put her mother-in-law, and James and his newfound religion, on Pause.

Sara set a square pan of hot gingerbread on a trivet and pulled off the oven mitts. "How'd I do?" She beamed at the woman with the steel gray hair pulled back in a painfully severe bun.

"Perfect." Bessie Tippet dabbed at her temples with the hem of her apron. Bumpy arthritic fingers pulled a flour sack towel off her shoulder and began wiping a glass plate. "Better than mine, actually."

"Never."

Bessie held the plate up to the light. "Did you chill the beaters?"

Sara opened the double-wide stainless steel refrigerator. She took a pint of whipping cream off a shelf and pointed to the crockery bowl and beaters next to it.

"Good girl."

The front door buzzer sounded as she plugged in the mixer. The timing was just right. Bessie would show the first

Friday night guests to the Tremayne Room. As soon as they were settled, they'd come downstairs and join their hostess for warm gingerbread and Devonshire tea in the spacious kitchen. And Sara would slip away to her pile of decorating magazines in the third-floor maid's quarters until nine, when it was time to fix the "Hearthside Hot Chocolate" and shortbread cookies Tippet House was famous for.

Bessie went to answer the door, and Sara did a quick mental tour of the house. She'd spent the morning scrubbing claw-footed bathtubs, making hospital corners on flowered sheets, and arranging lace-trimmed pillows in Glen, Penrose, Brae, and Tremayne, the four upstairs guestrooms. Since noon she'd cleaned five fireplaces and stacked them with fresh wood, baked four-dozen shortbread cookies and two pans of gingerbread. There wasn't a single fingerprint left on the refrigerator or stove.

Stiff peaks topped the sweetened cream when Bessie walked back into the kitchen, dabbing her top lip with a tissue. Her face was flushed.

"Are you all right?"

"Right as rain." Bessie straightened the lunch cloth on the table. "I've got some paperwork to get to. Would you mind being the hostess tonight?"

Sara glanced down at her baggy-kneed jeans and the bleached spot on her purple sweatshirt. It could all be covered with the white apron that hung on the back of the door. "Of course."

"There will be two couples coming around six. The man who just came is a businessman headed to International Falls. Just here for the night. Doesn't seem like much of a talker." Bessie picked up a list of local restaurants and fanned her face with it as she examined the sugar spoon for spots. "Does that make you uncomfortable?"

"Finding words isn't a big problem with mc. It'll be good practice."

"Then I'll see you in the morning."

Bessie walked into the back bedroom that doubled as her office, and Sara filled a cream pitcher. She'd just set it on the table when she heard footsteps descending the curved staircase and walking through the parlor. She grabbed the apron, slipped it over her head, and was just tying it around her waist when she froze.

"Reece!"

&

The last time she'd seen the six-foot-plus sandy blond bass player was just over two years ago. She'd handed her husband's ex–best friend an ice pack on his way out the door.

"Hi, Sara."

"What. . . ?" The last she'd heard, Reece Landon was in New York City

"You're still the only woman I've met under eighty who wears an apron." He grinned and shook his head. "I'd say I was just passing through, but I don't imagine you'd believe that."

He'd come to see her. Just what was she expected to say to that? She couldn't deny it was a scenario she'd toyed with more than once. Sara pulled out a chair and sank into it, motioning for him to do the same. "Would you. . .like some gingerbread?" That would buy her a few minutes to figure out if she was glad to see him. Could Reece Landon possibly do anything but complicate her life even more?

"Did you bake it?" Reece shrugged out of his sport coat and hung it on the back of the chair. "Nobody bakes like you."

Sara nodded, pretending her face didn't feel like she'd just opened the oven. "It's still warm. And there's homemade whipped cream."

A gentle, rolling laugh accompanied Reece's "I'd love some." He stretched his long legs out under the table. "If you're not too stingy on the whipped cream."

Sara stood and walked over to the counter, relieved to have

a reason to turn her back. She cut a larger-than-usual piece of cake and loaded it with whipped cream. As the spoon clattered back against the side of the bowl, she realized the gesture would send a message she didn't want to send. Or did she? It was too late to second-guess now. She set the plate in front of him.

"Thank you." His gaze latched on hers as he picked up his fork.

"Still take your coffee black?" She opened the cupboard and took down a mug. Reece Landon wasn't a teacup kind of man.

He nodded, smiled around his first bite, and winked. "Delicious."

Sitting down across from him, Sara didn't even try to disguise her curiosity. "You've changed." It wasn't just the haircut, the close shave, or sport coat.

"A little older." He rubbed his left hand across the knuckles of his right. "And much wiser."

"How is your hand?"

"It tells me when the weather's changing." He took another bite of gingerbread. Sara let the silence hang, sensing there was more he wanted to say. After he swallowed, he shook his head slowly. "Always wondered what would have happened if I'd hit his chin instead of your wall."

Sara allowed a fraction of a smile. "If his little girls couldn't keep him home, I don't think a fist in his face would have done it." She spread her hand on the tablecloth, not close enough to actually touch him. "I never got to thank you for trying to keep my family together. You lost your best friend over my marriage."

Reece shrugged. "Hey, I had a few principles even back then. I couldn't partner with a guy who'd leave his wife and kids." His hand closed over hers for a moment then dropped to his knee. "Have you managed okay, Sara?"

Trying to focus on anything but the brief warmth of his

skin on hers, she told him about getting into the Sanctuary program and about the fire that had started in the apartment above hers. She described life with the elderly lady who'd taken them in and how she'd finally gotten out on her own in a tiny rented mobile home that was destroyed by a tornado just months later. "And here I am. Back to taking handouts. Back to waking up grateful but angry every morning."

She described her plans to take over managing the bed-and-breakfast in Stillwater. When his gently probing questions about how she was coping threatened to crack the veneer she'd worked so hard to layer over raw emotions, she turned the spotlight on to him. "What are you doing now?"

"I'm living in the Cities and managing the cabins our family owns in International Falls. We're building three more cabins not far from here."

"You. . .working for your dad? This is not the Reece I once knew."

A sheepish smile parted his lips. "I used to be ashamed of my family's money. But I've figured out that if you don't make it an idol, it's pretty handy stuff to have."

"Tell me about it."

"You know. . ." Reece leaned forward. "I might have a job opportunity for you."

"Oh, really."

"I need somebody local to show properties and take reservations. I may have one person, but I could use two." He smiled as if there were some inside joke attached to his offer. "I could use someone with your obsessive-compulsive list-making tendencies."

Sara wrinkled her nose. "What makes you think I'm still a list maker?"

Reece nodded toward the open spiral notebook on the desk behind him. "I recognized the handwriting. Are you for hire?"

"Thanks, but I love what I'm doing." She eased away until

her back rested on the chair. "Are you still with a band?"

"No." Reece set his fork down. "Well, no and yes. I still play, but now it's with the worship team at my church."

Church? Worship band? *Reece?* A gear locked in Sara's brain, making another thought impossible.

He laughed. "I know. Who woulda thunk it, huh? I found the Lord about a year and a half ago." He set his napkin on the table and pushed his plate aside. "And a few months ago I had the privilege of leading your husband to Christ."

The gear dislodged, sending questions ricocheting in her head. The front doorbell buzzed just as she harnessed one fact and clung to it. One reality that made her stomach lurch.

Reece wasn't here to *see* her. He was here to convert her.

❧

They hadn't had another moment alone after the next guests arrived. Reece left for International Falls right after breakfast on Saturday yet still managed to follow her around all weekend. As Sara drove away from Tippet House just after four on Sunday, the look in Reece's eyes as she'd served hot chocolate, chatted with the guests, and set out the quiche-like *sformatino* for breakfast, still clawed at her insides. He'd stared at her the same way Mattie and her daughter Sydney and Audrey, the pastor's wife, looked at her—as if she were lost. It was straight-up pity, the kind of look Sara would give a toddler in the grocery store who'd strayed from her mother.

As if Reece setting up camp in her head wasn't enough of a strain, Bessie had acted weird all weekend, staying in her room much of the time and pushing Sara to do things she hadn't been trained to do. It had been good experience hosting breakfast, taking phone reservations, and being the go-to person for the guests, but Sara didn't appreciate the dump-her-in-the-deep-end education. Bessie was planning a trip to visit her sister in Arizona in February, and this was probably her way of being sure Sara could handle it all. But she could have given a bit of warning.

She turned onto the highway. Orange light flickered between the pines, stretching long, thin shadows across the snow-swirled road. Sara turned on the radio. Connie would bring the girls home at five on the dot, and she needed to have her head in a much better place by then. Kenny Chesney was in the middle of "Better as a Memory." The irony almost made her smile. Almost but not quite. "*Move on. . .Walk away. . .I'm just a dreamer. . . .*" James had made her "better as a memory" list long before he'd actually walked out the door. Maybe she'd add Reece to the lineup now.

Had it really been only five years since James and Reece had walked into Perk Place and rearranged her life? She'd been nineteen, overconfident, and way too flirty for her own good. She'd just finished her first year of interior design at the Art Institute in Mendota Heights and was home for the summer, holding down two jobs to earn money for tuition. Her mother had remarried and moved to Wyoming, so Sara was sleeping on a friend's futon on the floor. Her days were spent baking and waiting on customers at the coffee shop, her nights in the kitchen of the Sage Stoppe, Pine Bluff's only upscale restaurant, owned, at the time, by Bessie Tippet.

She could still see the two of them walking through the door in their leather jackets and faded jeans. There was something European about their appearance. Later she'd learned that it was a long-calculated look, designed to impress the agent they hoped to sign with.

Sara hadn't been the only one to take notice. The other girl working behind the counter had voiced out loud the sigh in Sara's mind. "I get the tall blond," she'd whispered. That was fine with Sara. Her eyes were riveted to the dark-haired one with the strong square jaw and sky blue eyes. The men both ordered pumpkin pie. Funny how a little thing like whipped cream could turn a man's head.

Just like Kenny Chesney's song, James had let her know early on that he wasn't interested in anything serious. He had a dream—a dream that included an agent in Canada and gigs in Liverpool and London. A dream that didn't include a waitress in Pine Bluff, Minnesota. "*Move on. . .Walk away. . . I'm just a dreamer. . . .*" Instead of listening, the challenge only made the chase that much sweeter. And she'd won, for a while. . . .

The song ended, and Sara turned off the radio. She couldn't risk another memory fueler. She turned her thoughts to her girls. These weekends away from them were hard. Missing them was a constant ache. She didn't feel quite whole without their chatter. Sunday night supper was a celebration and always the same—generic frozen pizza with instant chocolate pudding for dessert. The girls fought over stirring the pudding, ending up with far more on them than in the bowl. Sunday nights ended with a bubble bath and scrubbing the kitchen from top to bottom.

She was smiling when she turned onto Wright Avenue. But it didn't last long.

Reece Landon stood on her front porch.

She'd given him her address. He'd said he wanted to keep in touch. This wasn't what she thought he had in mind. Her legs felt tired and heavy as she got out of the car and walked toward him.

He was smiling, but it didn't hide that look of pity. "I wanted to say good-bye before I head home. And I was kind of hoping to see the girls."

Sara nodded. She wasn't mad at him. He hadn't, after all, tried to preach at her. . .or given her a tract with flames on it. Her disappointment had come from her own foolish ideas when he'd walked into the kitchen and looked at her in a way that made her feel significant. In a way that made her feel like something more than just a mom. She opened the front door, and he followed her into the hallway. "I can't ask you in. It's stupid, but it's house rules. Brock is the only guy who can be here since he's family, unless there are other people around."

Reece pulled his stocking cap off and then his gloves. "That's a good rule."

He *had* changed. "The girls will be back any minute."

In the awkward silence, Sara motioned toward the steps leading to the second floor. "Have a seat." She unlocked the door to her apartment. "I'll get some coffee." Raising her voice to be heard over the reverberating bass of rap music from one of the upstairs apartments, she pointed toward the source of the noise. "That's also against the rules."

His hands in air guitar position, Reece shook his head in time to the beat of the bass. Now this was the Reece she knew. When he stopped, he was laughing. "Don't bother with coffee. I can't stay long." His hand touched her shoulder. "I just can't leave without saying something face-to-face."

Here it comes. The salvation pitch. Sara closed her eyes and sighed, then she opened them and stared, waiting for the inevitable.

"Give James a chance. He's not the same guy who walked out on you. And he loves you, Sara."

Without warning, tears stung her eyes. Her throat tightened. *He loves you.* Those were words she couldn't afford to believe. Tears slipped over her lashes, and she swiped at them with a gloved hand.

Reece's arms wrapped around her. He pressed her head to his wool coat. She felt the roughness of his chin against her hair—

The front door opened. Connie Lewis stepped into the foyer.

four

Only one eye open, James groped for the insistent phone. In the red glow of his alarm clock—1:01 a.m.—he read the caller ID. His mother had never quite grasped the time difference between Pine Bluff, Minnesota, and London, England. It would be a nice respectable 7:01 p.m. back home.

" 'Ello, Mother." He salted his greeting with a heavy British beat, just to irritate her. He was letting her off pretty easily for waking him up after only an hour of sleep.

"James." She said it like a reprimand. As usual.

"What's up?"

"I just got home from taking the girls back."

He sat up and flipped the switch on his lava lamp. "Are they okay?"

"I. . .don't know."

His eyes were wide open now. "What's wrong? What happened?"

"I caught your wife making out with Reece Landon."

Making out? Nobody says "making out" anymore. His brain stuck on the seventies vocabulary before wrapping around the scene she was describing—his once–best friend kissing the woman he was, at least legally, still married to.

"James. It's time to end this. File for divorce and full custody, and come home and take care of your children. They need stability. She's bounced them around from place to place, and who knows how many men she's had living with her. It's not healthy."

Questions churned and multiplied like a mushroom cloud. Other men? Did his mother know of others? Reece and Sara together? It shouldn't surprise him. They'd hit it off from the beginning. It wouldn't take much to turn it into something deeper. Sara had to be lonely, and she owed him nothing. But Reece? The guy who had come all the way to England to hunt him down? The guy who had shown him what a Jesus-following, changed-from-the-inside man looks like?

Sara's unfaithfulness he could justify. Reece's betrayal was a knife to the gut.

Then again, Reece had just called him about the job opening back home. What was that all about? Wasn't there a saying about keeping your friends close and your enemies closer? "What did you see?" He really only wanted an answer if it was better than where his thoughts were leading.

"You heard me. I walked in the door with the girls, and there they were—going at it, totally oblivious to the rest of the world."

Pressing his thumb and forefinger against his eyes didn't black out the vision. *Lord, I deserve this, I know I do, but. . . But what? But turn back the clock? Make it like it never happened? Like I was never so caught up in myself that I destroyed the best thing I ever had?*

"Do you know anything more? Did Sara explain anything? Are they living together?"

"I assume so. She didn't explain a thing. After I'd watched your girls for three long days, all she could say was 'Get your hands off my children.'"

❧

Chocolate pudding splattered the table, the wall, the floor, and Sara, but the girls were clean, read to, and sound asleep. Rinsing the ragged dishcloth for the second time, Sara stared at the chocolate-tinted water rushing toward the drain. Slowly it turned milky brown then clear again.

Wash it away. Why couldn't she just wash it away? Zoe's fear-filled eyes as Connie pulled her back toward the car. Sadie's mittened hand stretching out to her. "Mommy!"

Never in her life had Sara moved so fast. Out the door,

down the steps, one arm grabbing Sadie while the fingers of her other hand latched onto Zoe's jacket hood. But Connie didn't let go. She kept moving, her back to Sara, toward her car.

"Get your hands off my children!"

"No. You've crossed the line this time."

Sara folded the pudding-smeared cloth over on itself. *This time?* What other imaginary lines had she crossed?

With the flood of "what-ifs" rushing through the center of her brain, she couldn't grapple with that question right now. What if Reece hadn't stepped in to pull Sadie out of Connie's arms while Sara untangled Zoe's fingers from her mother-in-law's clutch? What if Allison was right and Connie really did want to take her girls away from her?

Icy tendrils of fear tightened around her chest. What could she say in court that would hold up against all that James's parents had to offer? Their old farmhouse on two acres between Pine Bluff and North Branch was equivalent to Disney World in her girls' eyes. Brock had built the most elaborate backyard playground Sara had ever seen—two sandboxes, a kiddie pool, three slides, swings of every height, rings and ropes, and a teeter-totter. Inside the house, the girls had their own room. Purple, pink, and sparkles. Nothing faded. Nothing secondhand.

Her girls were well fed, healthy, and secure, and anyone could see they were happy. Yet for the past few nights, Sara had awakened in a cold sweat after a dream that almost became reality just hours ago. Sometimes Connie stood at her door demanding her children, sometimes uniformed officers with guns. She'd rehearsed her lines over and over in her sleep. *They're mine! You can't take them! Get your hands off my children!*

Filling the sink with water and detergent, she watched three plastic bowls rise on the tide, slowly fill, and capsize. Bubbles swept across the surface of the water until the bowls were hidden from view.

He loves you, Sara.

Only in the books that littered the floor in the next room did the prince come home to rescue the princess with his undying love. In real life, love dies.

Give James a chance.

What if that was the only way to keep the girls?

He's not the same guy who walked out on you.

Bubbles glistened, clean and pristine. Sara fished for a capsized bowl. Beneath the white froth, the water had turned murky brown.

Maybe not so different from a man who claims he's not what he used to be.

≈

A soft glow lit the room. The three-foot Christmas tree in the corner boasted two strings of colored lights and a dozen frosted sugar cookies hung by red yarn. Sara pulled a blanket off the back of the couch, wrapped it around herself, and sat down, wedging her feet between the cushions. No point staying in bed if all she was going to do was fight with covers and memories.

She'd drifted off for a few minutes, long enough to dream about James. Strange that her dreams of him were always good ones. In this one he'd brought her a small white bag with a snowman face on the front. She'd opened it and found a fresh sprig of mistletoe. His kiss woke her.

Sara breathed on cupped hands. The blanket wasn't doing a thing against the chill in the room. She picked up the tablet of paper she'd left on the arm of the sofa. Bessie had asked her to plan menus for next weekend's breakfasts. Meat-and-potato-stuffed Cornish pasties and raspberry-filled meringues were a better use of her time than thoughts of James. And mistletoe.

She heard the front door of the building open then close. Raquel, her neighbor across the hall, getting home from her second-shift job. Sara stared at the clock then at the Christmas tree. As the idea took shape, she threw off the blanket. Opening the apartment door, she ran across the hall and tapped her knuckles on the door.

"Who is it?" Raquel's cigarette-roughened voice came through the door.

"Sara. I want to ask you something."

The door opened wide. "Hey. C'mon in." Raquel pulled a rubber band from her ponytail. Rusty brown hair straggled to her shoulders. She smiled, deepening the laugh lines surrounding her lips. Life had aged her beyond her thirty-nine years. "Thanks for the cookies. I got a few before Allison nabbed 'em. She's eating like a horse these days. Oh, and thanks for the card last week."

"Six months sober is something to celebrate."

"Yeah." Raquel's chin lifted. "It is. So what's up?"

"I have a huge, huge favor to ask of you and Allison." Sara's mind whirled, thinking as she talked. She stared at the beige couch against the bare beige walls. "Remember how you said you wanted to paint?"

Raquel's confusion was accompanied by a yawn. "We'd be doing you a favor if we painted our living room?"

Sara laughed. "No. I'd be doing you a favor by painting your living room. And your bedroom and bathroom and Allison's room and anything else you can think of."

"And we'd be doing what?"

"Watching my girls on the weekends."

❧

James sat on the narrow, thin mattress of the iron-framed bed, staring at his checkbook register. The timing was perfect; finances weren't. With the money he'd get for playing his final night at the tavern, he could just squeak by without touching the check he'd been carrying in his wallet for weeks. As long as he didn't plan on eating along the way.

It wouldn't be the first time he'd traveled on empty.

Lord, stop me if I shouldn't be doing this. Throw a roadblock in my way if I'd just be making things worse.

He waited, listening to the traffic rumbling over the cobblestones below, feeling the low vibration from the Tube, London's subway, far beneath him. As usual at three o'clock, the cat lady in the flat directly above him began vacuuming her rugs. He didn't sense the voice of God in all the clamor. He picked up his phone and punched 2.

"Lewis residence. Brock speaking."

James rolled his eyes. Brock the chameleon. Enough of Brock's antics had leaked to James to let him know his little brother wasn't the sweet boy his mama bragged about, and yet, at nineteen, Brock was still playing the charade at home to ensure free room and board while he commuted to school. How could two people who shared so much DNA be so completely different? At nineteen, James had left home to see the world. . .and found all he wanted in a coffee shop in Pine Bluff. All he'd wanted for a while, anyway.

"Brock. I have a favor to ask."

"What?" His brother sounded wary.

"Pick me up at the airport on Saturday."

five

The pale light of December dawn filtered through the thin pink curtain as Sara brushed feathery kisses over the girls' foreheads. This was going to be so much easier than waking them and listening to their sleepy whines as she prodded them to get dressed and ready for Grandma Connie.

Coffee mug in hand, she padded across the hallway and knocked on the door. "Allison? You up?" She kept her voice low. The single moms in the two upstairs apartments wouldn't appreciate their kids being roused.

The door creaked open. Allison hugged a pillow and blanket. Her hair looked like it hadn't made friends with a brush in days. Dark-smudged eyes blinked from her puffy face. "Morning."

"Are you feeling okay?"

Allison nodded. "Just a little queasy. I'll be fine by the time they wake up." She stepped into the hallway and shut the door behind her. "Anything I gotta know?"

"I left a note on the table about food and their bedtime routine."

"Okay." Allison rubbed her hand over her stomach. Her face looked pale. She nodded, shuffled into Sara's apartment, and flopped down on the couch.

Sara took a deep breath, then another. In spite of the cold wood floor beneath her socks, she felt clammy. *They'll be fine.* As long as her mother-in-law didn't decide to show up while she was at work and take matters—take her girls—into her own hands. The girls had asked why they weren't going to Grandma Connie's, but they'd accepted Sara's white lie about Allison wanting to play with them. Sara half expected to find

Crazy Connie waiting on the porch.

She opened the front door just wide enough to stick out her arm. The sudden cold was a shock. Her hand darted toward her mailbox. For a split second, her damp fingertips stuck to the metal flap. She pulled out the bundle of yesterday's mail. It was thicker than usual.

Shutting the door and leaning against it, she slurped the last of her coffee and hung the mug on her little finger. She opened the top envelope and stared down at a picture of a squinty-eyed newborn. Inscribed below it was the birth announcement. *Trace and Sydney McKay proudly introduce their son, Benjamin Eldon McKay. . . .*

Tears prickled the rims of Sara's eyes. She wasn't quite sure why. Joy was part of it; new babies just did that to her. But maybe a smidgen of it was sadness. She'd probably never give birth to a son.

Shaking her head, she took another deep breath. Leaving the girls for three days was hard enough; she didn't need to start manufacturing new reasons to be sad. The next envelope was a letter from her mother and stepfather. She'd take that along to savor during her morning break. The third thing in the pile was a 6 x 8 padded envelope. The minute her hand closed around the stack of mail in the box, she'd known what was in it. The book. The book that was going to teach her how to put on a string of pearls and her best little dress and light the candles and meet her husband at the door—*Recipe for a Godly Wife.*

I tried that, James. Don't you remember? Oh no, that's right, you wouldn't. That was the night you never came home.

&

"Is there a good Bible-based church in the area?" The pewter-haired woman with the black pearls and crocheted pink sweater took a plate of scones from Sara and smiled sweetly.

Weren't all churches based on the Bible? Wasn't that the definition of a church? Sara took a dish of lemon curd off the tray in her hand and set it on the table. "Pineview Community Church is a good one. The people are very friendly." Not that she'd ever gone to a church service, but she'd met Pastor Owen and the Sanctuary volunteers.

"Is that where you go?" The pearl lady's expression seemed to combine both hope and pity, as if Sara's answer would tell her what kind of smile was appropriate.

"Actually, every Sunday's like today. I work until four." She realized that wasn't giving the woman the information she sought. There'd likely be a tract under the cup and saucer when she cleared the dining room table. She just hoped there'd be no flames. "I'll get you the brochure for the church."

She walked through the swinging saloon-type doors into the kitchen. Bessie stood with her back against the counter, a rose-covered teapot dangling carelessly from one hand. The other hand was clamped over her mouth.

"Bessie?" Sara set her tray down and made three quick steps, grabbing the teapot. "What's wrong?"

It seemed to take an effort for Bessie to focus on Sara. When she did, she took a tremulous breath. "I. . .need to talk to you. . .after they leave." She blinked then wiped her hands on her apron. "I. . .don't want to keep you right now." She nodded stiffly toward the dining room.

Sara's pulse picked up tempo, tapping on her eardrums. She nodded. "I'll fill the pot." Knees stiff, she walked to the stove. Steam dampened her bangs as she filled the rose-patterned pot with the kettle. Her mind whirled with questions. What had she done? Bessie had never given the slightest indication that she was unhappy with her performance. But what if. . . Steam stung her nostrils as she tried to breathe the thought away. What if Connie had talked to Bessie? Things like integrity and character mattered immensely to Bessie. If Connie had told her about finding Reece at her door, if she'd painted the picture she'd created in her imagination. . . Sara put the cover on the teapot, pulled a brochure from the rack over the kitchen desk, and fabricated a smile as she walked into the dining room.

"How is everything?" She made eye contact with each of the six people seated at the table—two sixty-something couples on a getaway weekend from the Cities and a couple on their honeymoon. Murmurs of approval came from all six. Sara pulled out the chair at the head of the table.

The young bride, Lydia, passed the plate of pasties to her. "Did you make these?"

Sara took one of the half-circle pies. The crust around the edge was perfectly browned and showed Sara's unique crimp, slightly deeper and more angled than Bessie's. The savory smell wafted from the vents she'd cut in the top. "I did. Do you like them?"

"I love them."

"Tradition claims that the pasty was originally made by the women of Cornwall for their men who worked in the tin mines. They'd be covered with dirt from the mines with no way to wash before lunch, so they would hold the pasty by the thick edge and eat the rest without touching it. The crust they threw away was supposed to appease the spirits who might otherwise lead miners into danger."

"That's fascinating."

"The Cornish who came to Minnesota to work in the iron mines brought their traditions with them. Bessie Tippet's great-grandfather was one of them."

"I love history." Lydia winked at her husband and turned back to Sara. "Are pasties hard to make?"

"Not at all. The trick to making the crust is to use real lard, and the secret to the filling is to dice the potatoes and rutabagas just the right size. I'll give you the recipe before you leave."

"I'd love that."

Love. It seemed to be the girl's only verb. No wonder,

looking at the deep brown eyes adoring her, the arm resting protectively along the back of her chair. Sara cut into her pasty, needing something to do other than stare at the two who were in their own world even as they interacted with the other guests.

She remembered the feeling, remembered James looking at her as if she were his whole world. For a while.

The woman with the black pearls held out a plate of scones. "These simply melt in your mouth. I can't imagine why you're so skinny. You'd think you'd have to taste everything to cook like this." She patted Sara's arm and whispered, "You need to taste more. A stiff wind could blow you away."

"Thank you." Sara took a scone, leaving it to the woman to decide if she was thanking her for the scone or the comment.

Black Pearl's husband leaned forward. "Is there a book on the history of Pine Bluff?"

Sara nodded, wiping her mouth with her napkin. She got up and went into the kitchen. As she picked up the book—*Growing Up in Pine Bluff*—she glanced at Bessie's back. The woman stood, spine straight as a white pine, facing the window that looked out on the gazebo in the backyard, now covered with the four inches of new snow that had fallen during the night. Bessie didn't turn around.

Sara walked back into the dining room and filled the hour with stories she'd learned from the book in her hand and from the woman who stood silently in the kitchen, waiting to talk to her.

❧

It was just after noon when she pulled onto the highway. It seemed all wrong to be leaving Tippet House so early.

It was. All wrong.

Tears she'd held in for hours broke loose. Sara pulled the car to the side of the road and sobbed.

"Where is your God now, James?"

The question hung in the air with her breath. Cold, crystal, visible for a moment then gone. Was God watching her? Breaking her down, inch by inch? Waiting for the moment when she'd had enough punishment?

She flashed back to the night of the fire. She'd heard a noise, like crinkling paper, and then a loud *pop*. Out in the hallway she smelled smoke. *Please God, protect us.* She woke the girls, ran upstairs. Smoke seeped from under the door of the empty apartment above hers. Somehow she'd managed to get everyone out of the building, run across the street, and call 9-1-1. But God hadn't answered her prayer that night. The little girl upstairs had needed skin grafts, and smoke damage kept all of them from returning to their apartments.

The next scene filled the screen in her private horror show—huddling in the cement-block laundry building, covering the girls with her arms like a hen with chicks, listening to the roar of the approaching tornado. . . . *Please God. . .keep them safe.* But their trailer had been flattened; their clothes scattered; furniture, appliances, pictures ruined.

Sara pressed the heels of her hands against her eyes. This time she wouldn't pray. This time, like the others, nothing could fix it. The movie in her head zoomed in on Bessie, staring out at the gazebo, talking in a strange and distant voice. . . . *Rheumatoid arthritis getting worse. . .I can't do this anymore. . . . I'm moving to Arizona. . .already listed the house. . . . I'm sorry, Sara. . .so sorry.*

Heat whispered from the vents, and she could no longer see her breath. Sara put the car in gear. Snow crunched beneath her tires as she eased her rust-marred car onto the road. *We'll be okay. I'll find a job.* She still had two checks coming. The letter from her mother had included money for Christmas gifts for the girls. She'd tuck it away just in case. *We'll be okay.*

At the gas station on Main Street, she picked up the Sunday *Star Tribune* and the weekly Pine Bluff paper. If she was lucky, Sadie would be ready for a nap when she got home and Zoe would spend her "quiet time" hour actually being quiet. And Sara could comb through the classifieds.

Throwing the three-inch-thick Minneapolis paper on the seat, she thought of Mattie's "Bounce Award." She had to bounce back one more time. Enough to get her credit card paid off so that her earnings at the Stillwater Inn could be put toward one thing alone—the land contract payments that would make the castle hers someday.

"One more time." She said the words but didn't feel them. She had to do it, had to find the drive to look for a job, to pare her budget. Again. Her back was against the ropes, but self-pity would weaken her. She couldn't, even for a moment, cave into it, because there was no way she was going to give her mother-in-law reason to take her girls. That thought dried her tears until she turned onto Wright Avenue and saw Connie's car parked in front of her building.

"One more time." Sara parked the car, got out, pulled her bags out of the backseat, and squared her shoulders. With determined steps, she walked up the porch steps and opened the front door. With her hand on the doorknob of her apartment, she stopped, took a moment to gather her resolve. Of all the people in the world she didn't want to see in this frame of mind, Connie Lewis topped the list.

She opened the door. . .and gasped. There was one name above Connie's on that list.

And he sat in her living room. . .reading a book to his daughters.

six

She was so thin. That was the first thing James noticed. The second was that she'd been crying. A sickening sense of déjà vu tightened his gut.

Brock had told him not to come to the apartment, but he'd also let it slip that Sara wouldn't be home until five. He just needed a few minutes with the girls to be sure they were all right. And he wanted to show up before Reece knew he was in town and had time to pack and leave. He had to know if any of what his mother had told him in the last twenty-four hours was true.

Sadie wriggled off his lap and ran to Sara, wrapping herself around her leg.

Zoe waved. "We're reading *Goodnight Moon*."

The babysitter, who'd been watching his every move and refusing to answer his questions, stepped out of the kitchen. "I called Brock at work, and he said I could let him in."

Sara nodded. James knew that look. Every fiber of her being was fighting to hold herself in check. "Thank you, Allison. Tell your mom thanks."

The teen slowly gathered her things and ambled out of the apartment, probably hoping something interesting would happen before she left.

Sara didn't move. In one hand she held a purse, in the other a large canvas bag. She hadn't acknowledged Sadie, who was wrapped around her thigh like a firefighter sliding down a pole.

James bent his head toward Zoe. "Let's finish this later. I want to talk to your mommy."

"Okay." Zoe slid off the couch and ran into another room.

Sara finally dropped her bag, picked up Sadie, and hugged her, burying her face in the flyaway corn silk–colored hair. "I missed you, princess. Go help Zoe make placemats for supper."

"Pizza. . .pudding. . .pizza. . .pudding. . .pizza!" Sadie ran off, singing her made-up song.

James stood, took three steps, and stopped. After all the times he'd rehearsed this moment, he couldn't think of a thing to say. "Sara."

Her teeth bit down on her bottom lip. Her eyes burned into him.

"I should have called first." The words sounded so lame.

"Yes."

"Could—" He swallowed. His tongue felt like stone. "Could we talk?"

She walked toward a worn and faded chair. Her movements were robotic. She lowered herself to the chair and folded her hands on her lap.

James sat down on the couch and angled toward her, resting his elbows on his knees. Like her, he folded his hands. *Lord, tell me what to say.* To give her some emotional space, he looked away. His gaze landed on the book he'd sent her, lying open like a tent, pages bent, beside her chair. As if it had been thrown there.

He wiped his hands on his knees and refolded them. "The girls are beautiful."

Sara nodded. Her expression was no longer angry. It was vacant. Dead, unfeeling.

"You've done a wonderful job raising them."

Again she nodded, still with no emotion he could read. He'd rather deal with her anger than this.

"I know that saying I'm sorry isn't going to mean a thing to you. I don't have a single excuse for putting my wants ahead of you and the girls, and I can't ever make it up to you."

He looked at her blank stare and considered getting up

and walking out the door—for her sake. She didn't need him stirring up old pain. He parted his hands and rested them beside him. One hand fell on *Goodnight Moon*. The feeling of holding his daughters on his lap came back with a wave of pain like circulation to frostbitten toes. "It would be wrong of me to ask for another chance. But would it be possible for us to spend some time talking? Just to see if maybe—"

Fear replaced her dead stare and silenced him. Nothing was coming out right. He studied the shadows under her eyes and her pale but still flawless skin. She wore no makeup and was dressed in faded jeans and a denim jacket that had once been black. Like her, the jacket was too thin. White lines showed on the edge of the cuffs where the fabric had worn away. So different from the clothes-conscious girl with the heavy eye makeup he'd fallen for five years ago. That girl had been spunky and pretty. This one was strong and hauntingly beautiful. In spite of the coldness in her eyes, everything in him longed to know this woman.

He held his breath, waiting for her answer.

Sara's eyes closed. Her shoulders rose in a heavy sigh. "What would that accomplish?"

৵

His nod was barely perceptible. As desperately as Sara wanted to look away from the hurt on his face, she couldn't. His eyes glistened and he blinked. Bending down, he picked up his jacket. She hadn't seen it on the floor behind the coffee table. At the sight of the scarred brown leather, her pulse skipped. She tried not to remember the scent of it but couldn't block it out.

He stood up, slid his arms into the jacket. He hadn't said a word after her reply. Sara rose to her feet but couldn't have moved away from that spot if she'd wanted to. Her legs felt nailed to the floor. Reece had told the truth—this was not the same man who walked out on her. His body had filled out, and his face had lost its boyish look. A long-sleeved black T-shirt fit tight across well-defined muscles. She wondered how he could move his arms in the snug jacket. The sky blue eyes she saw in her dreams seemed deeper set and held the look of a man who had lived hard for the past two years.

As he zipped his jacket, he looked at her with a slight smile that hinted of regret. "I'll be at Mom and Dad's until the day after Christmas if. . ." Leaving the sentence unfinished, he walked past her then turned and reached out to her. The back of his hand touched her cheek. His eyes gleamed with tears. "Sara. . ." His voice was soft and hoarse, just above a whisper. "I still love you."

He took his gloves from the shelf and walked out the door.

❧

Her hands shook. Her whole body vibrated with the shock of finding James in her living room, looking so natural, so comfortable with her girls.

For two years she'd imagined the moment she'd have to face him. For some reason, she'd always pictured it at his mother's funeral years from now. The girls would be grown and successful in whatever they chose to do, proving she'd been a good mom after all. She'd be the owner of the Stillwater Inn, the B&B with the five-star reviews in travel magazines. Rich, happy, maybe even married to a man who put her above his career; she'd offer James her tastefully jeweled and manicured hand. "Hello, James," she'd say. Her voice would have just a hint of condescension, but no anger. She'd let him know she'd forgotten him long ago and that she and her daughters had done fine without him.

At times, she'd envisioned him groveling at her feet, begging her to take him back. That wasn't James, of course, but once in a while she needed to picture him fully aware of how much he'd missed. It took the edge off her bitterness.

Not once had she imagined him the way he was tonight. Physically stronger, yet emotionally vulnerable, focused more on her and the girls than on himself. Her chest tightened as she realized how close she'd come to falling into his arms, to believing he'd changed enough to make it work, to make it last.

But had he changed in the ways that would matter to her? Even if James was nicer, calmer, maybe even more attentive to her, he was still a musician. He'd always be a musician. She didn't know what he was doing in London, most likely still with a band. Maybe now he was with a Christian group, but that wouldn't make any difference. He'd still be engrossed in practicing and writing. Every conversation would roll around to his next gig or their next song that was destined to be at the top of the charts. There'd still be time on the road. . .time away from her.

Zoe ran out of the bedroom, stopping several feet from Sara's chair. Her little hands flew to her hips in a gesture that mirrored Sara's often-impatient stance. "Where did he go?"

Sara stood, realizing for the first time she was still wearing her jacket. "He went home." She took off her jacket and threw it on the couch, covering the spot where James had sat. "He went home."

"But we didn't finish *Goodnight Moon*."

"I'll read it to you before quiet time." A question rose in her mind. "Do you know who that man was?"

"Uh-huh." Zoe's curls bobbed. "He's Uncle Brock's friend. Can we have pizza now?"

He hadn't told her he was their daddy. The knowledge rocked her. "It's a long time until supper." Her voice held a quiver she couldn't control.

"But I'm starving!"

"Didn't you have lunch yet?"

"Nuh-uh."

Scooping her up, Sara planted a loud kiss on her cheek. "All right, my drama queen. Go get a box of pudding out of the cupboard, and tell Sadie to come help me with the pizza."

Zoe ran a few steps then stopped. "Can sometime that man eat pizza with us like Uncle Brock does?"

As Sara bent to pick up her jacket, she saw something on the floor beside the chair. The book she'd chucked across the room on Friday. The one that would tell her how to be a submissive little wife and smile and nod when her husband packed his bags to travel with the band for months at a time.

"No. That man lives far, far away."

❧

"Girls napping?" Raquel pulled out a kitchen chair and helped herself to a slice of room-temperature pizza.

Sara nodded, picking up a pudding-covered Winnie the Pooh spoon. "Zoe fell asleep, too. You must have worn them out this morning."

Raquel shrugged. "They went to Sunday school."

"*What?*"

"Yeah. Mattie picked us up. I'm kinda gettin' the 'higher power' stuff, so I figured I'd give the church thing a shot."

"But. . ." The spoon clattered into the sink. Sara turned. "I don't want them—"

"Cool it." Raquel rolled her eyes toward the ceiling. "They're too young to get brainwashed. They had a blast." She picked a chunk of green pepper off her pizza and set it on the counter. "So your ex showed up."

"My unofficial ex."

"I caught a glimpse. What a hunk. If Brock grows up that fine, Allison will be one lucky girl."

Sara's fingers tightened on the spoon. This wasn't the first time Raquel had implied that Brock had more than a platonic interest in her daughter. Since Allison had made it clear that she wouldn't be expecting anything from the baby's father, Raquel had set her sights on Brock. Though Brock and Allison had been friends for years, Sara couldn't imagine two people less suited to be life mates. Brock needed a woman with at least a little bit of ambition. On that one point she was sure she and her mother-in-law would agree. "They're just friends."

"Uh-huh." Biting into the pizza, Raquel grinned. "Wish I had a friend like that."

Before Sara could formulate a controlled answer, her front door opened. Brock walked in, knocking as he entered. Allison hovered behind him like a shadow. Brock's gaze swept the apartment. "He's not here, is he?"

"No." Sara threw her dish towel on her shoulder, walked across the room, and gave her brother-in-law a hug. "Missed you, kid."

"They got me working weird hours this month." Brock returned her hug with his right arm. More than a year after the car accident that killed his best friend, he was still in therapy for his reconstructed shoulder.

Allison sat on the couch, and Brock joined her, a little too close for Sara's liking. Without meaning to, she made eye contact with Raquel, who returned a look that clearly said, *See?* Sara looked away.

Brock tapped his fist against his knee. "I told James not to just show up. I knew you'd leave work early if you found out he was here."

Sara slumped into the chair. She didn't feel like talking about the real reason she'd left early.

"Did you kick him out?" Brock's eyes held a steely glint. Like Reece, he'd sided with her when James left for the second time. Young as he was, for two years now he'd been the father figure in her girls' lives.

Sara shook her head. "Do you think he's changed?"

"Yeah. Not for the better. He's off the wall about his religion. He sticks God into every conversation. It's weird."

Allison rested both hands on her slightly rounded belly. "He asked a lot of questions."

"What kind of questions?"

"About what you do and if you're seeing anyone and stuff like that."

Brock put his elbows on his knees and folded his hands, a posture that mirrored the man who'd sat in that same spot two hours earlier. "You know why he's here, don't you? Mom's been a raving lunatic since she caught you and Reece—"

"She didn't 'catch' us. We weren't doing anything."

Raquel jumped off the kitchen chair and perched on the end of the couch. "Who's Reece? What did I miss?"

Allison shifted to face her mother. "Crazy Connie walked in when Sara was kissing this cute guy who used to be a friend of Brock's brother."

Raquel clapped her hands together and winked at Sara. "What a life you got, girl!"

Sara covered her face with her dish towel and groaned. Knowing Raquel, half the town would hear an embellished version before the week was out. For a moment she teetered on the brink of laughter. Her life had become a soap opera. No, a country western song—lost her man, her job, her house. . .and now her reputation.

seven

"Don't let Mom find out." Brock walked through Raquel's living room on Tuesday afternoon with one girl wrapped around each leg. While they giggled, his eyes were fastened on Sara.

Looking down at the paint she'd just opened, she began to stir. "Your mother doesn't need to know. . .and neither does your brother. Do you understand? I'll find a job."

"Good luck. I'd get you in at the store, but everybody's coming home from college."

"I'll find something." Her voice reflected her doubt. She'd made six calls the day before. Not one place had even told her to pick up an application. The offer from Reece was probably still open. That would give Connie enough evidence to bury her. *And now she's working with the man I saw her kissing. . . .* "I'll get a job."

"You better. Mom's just waiting for you to mess up."

Her knuckles whitening around the stir stick, Sara froze. Evidently Allison hadn't fabricated her prediction. "Have you actually heard her say that she wants to take the girls from me?"

Brock looked cornered. "Yeah. She makes it sound like they're starving and neglected and she has to rescue them."

Sara's teeth ground together. A weight settled on her chest. "What makes her think she'd get them? Even if she could prove I was an unfit mother, who says the state wouldn't step in and put them in foster care or award them to my mother? Does she really think James would leave his music and move in with her so they could raise my kids like a happy little family? Doesn't she realize that he gave up his chance to—"

51

"I'm ready." Allison pranced out of her bedroom with her hat, gloves, and jacket on.

Sara looked from her to Brock. "Ready for what?" Brock and Allison had promised to watch the girls in her apartment while Sara painted Raquel's living room.

A mix of embarrassment and frustration crossed Brock's face. "Uh. . .we were thinking maybe of taking them for ice cream or hot chocolate. . .you know. I. . .didn't tell them yet, but I figured you'd be okay with it, you know. . . ."

Taking her hand off the stir stick, Sara set both hands on her hips. "Brock?"

He stopped walking, looked at her then down at the girls.

Since Sunday night, Sara had been waiting—for what, she wasn't sure. "Is *he* involved in this?"

Wide brown eyes stared back at her. "*He?*"

Sara's laugh was hollow. "You're a lousy actor, kid." She glanced at the girls. Engrossed in tickling each other, they weren't listening, but she wanted to be careful. "You were going to take them to see him without telling me, weren't you?"

"He's only here for a few weeks. You gotta let him spend some time with them."

"He'll see them on Christmas Day." She'd made that decision for the girls' sake, not for James's. She wouldn't be there, but she wouldn't take that tradition away from them. And James would be leaving the day after Christmas. She narrowed her eyes at Brock. "I thought you were on my side."

Brock dropped into a sheet-covered chair, and the girls scrambled onto his lap. "Why do there have to be sides?"

Sara simply stared at him, feeling suddenly alone. She'd lost her only ally in the family.

"We had a long talk last night." He finally looked her straight in the eye. "The religion stuff is annoying, but that's not the only change in him. Ja—*he* is really sorry about leaving you, Sara. And I kind of understand what was going on in his head. It wasn't really all his fault, you know. It makes more sense now that I heard the whole thing."

The emotion that took hold of her felt more like fire than anger. Her nerves seemed to literally burn, from her shoulders to her fingertips. "It makes *sense?*" Zoe and Sadie stopped tickling Brock and stared at her. She heard the front door open, but she didn't care who heard her yelling. "It makes *sense* that he left me to raise two kids without a father? It makes sense that—"

Brock turned toward the door, and she followed his gaze. The door that had been partway open for ventilation opened all the way.

James stood in the doorway. "You're right, Sara. None of it makes sense."

❧

He hadn't been prepared for the intensity of her rage. He knew she wouldn't be any happier to see him this time than she had been on Sunday, but with the clock ticking, he had to give it a shot. Maybe he was crazy for hoping she'd listen, but one thing was sure: If he didn't try, the guilt that had gnawed at his insides for the past two years would swallow him whole.

"Can we talk?" The same words hadn't gotten him anywhere two days ago.

Without taking her piercing gaze from him, she spoke to Brock. "Put the girls down for naps."

"Let's go, ladies." Brock handed Sadie to Allison.

As they were walking out, Zoe waved at James. "You said Uncle Brock's friend lived far, far away, Mommy."

"He does." Sara's tone was hard, her voice strained.

Zoe ran to Sara and threw her arms around her waist. "I'm just gonna have quiet time, right? I don't hafta sleep."

Sara nodded. James watched as Sadie copied her sister, squirming out of Allison's arms and running to hug Sara. He'd missed so much. What would their life be like if he'd stayed?

When Sara Martin and her amazing green eyes had snared him, he'd told the other band members to go on to Canada without him, said he'd join them in a few weeks. And he had. Without telling Sara he was leaving, he'd made the trip across the border in the middle of the night. . .just hours after she'd told him she was pregnant.

For weeks, he'd poured himself into his music, sure he'd forget her, convinced that she didn't really love him and that she and the baby would be better off without a guy who wasn't even close to husband or father material. But it didn't work. He hitchhiked back to Pine Bluff, married Sara, and gave up his dream for the next two years.

But Sara had never acknowledged what he'd given up or what he'd put his friends through for her.

Brock and Allison carried the girls across the hall, and the sheet-shrouded room was suddenly quiet. James took off his leather gloves and stuffed them in his pockets. The apartment was warm, but he didn't dare unzip his jacket. Sara needed to be the one to decide if he was staying. "I don't want to hash over old stuff. . .unless you do, I mean." He ran his hand across his jaw. He wasn't saying it the way it played in his head. "I need to explain something."

Her hands were on her hips, a pose only too familiar to James. She pointed to the paint buckets and the room around them and sighed. "I have to finish this tonight."

He nodded. No way would he leave that easily. Not this time. "I'll help."

Green eyes sparked like backlit emeralds. She'd painted their townhouse, every room, without him. She had to be wondering why he'd never offered when it mattered. Sara lifted the stir stick out of the paint can.

He'd seen that shade before. "Nice color."

A wistful expression crossed her face. For the briefest of moments, he could almost have called it a smile. "Bittersweet." Her tone melted to a softness that made his heart skip. "It's the same color I painted our bedroom."

"I know." *Bittersweet*. The irony made him match her almost smile. "I should have helped you."

His admission seemed to catch her off guard. He spotted a hint of vulnerability before she bent down for something beneath the newspaper-covered card table that held the paint. When she straightened, she held two things out to him—a paint roller and a trimmer.

She was letting him stay. It took monumental self-control to not grin at her like a two-year-old offered a triple-scoop cone. A tempered smile escaped as he reached for the roller. "You're good at the detail work."

Sara's cheeks seemed to flush, but she turned away so quickly that he wasn't sure if he'd imagined it. Was she that unaccustomed to compliments? The obvious answer fed the guilt monster. Unaccustomed to compliments from him, certainly. When had that stopped? Long before Sadie came along, he guessed.

He unzipped his jacket, walked out to the front entryway, and hung it on the newel post. Pushing up his sleeves, he went back to the card table and poured several inches of paint into a tray. "Brock told me what you've done for Allison's mom."

With a shrug, Sara dipped the trimmer pad into the tray. "Raquel and Allison watch the girls for me."

"I know." He'd heard more than he wanted to about that arrangement. His mother had done some private investigation work. "According to Brock, Allison's mom wouldn't be living here and certainly wouldn't be sober if it weren't for you."

This time, there was no question about the color that tinted her face. "Brock told me a friend of his and her mom needed a place to live. I just let them know when there was an opening."

James knew she'd done much more than that. She'd driven the woman to AA meetings, fixed decent meals for her, and showed her how to clean and organize. *That's my Sara*. The thought came spontaneously and with it a jab of regret. "She must be a completely different person than when you first met her." He hoped it sounded like a casual statement. He also hoped it would have an impact.

Sara stared at him, set the trimmer on the edge of the paint tray, and took a deep breath. After several seconds, she pointed at the couch. "Maybe we should move that out a little farther."

Strange what a simple, ordinary sentence could do to a guy. "Sure." He grabbed one end while she took the other. Since becoming a Christian, he'd met people who saw symbolism in everything. He wasn't one of them, but he couldn't ignore the picture of teamwork.

They set the couch about three feet from where it had been. Sara looked down at the floor and actually laughed. "*Bus. . .ted.*" She bent over and picked up an open package of peanut butter cookies and a bag of peppermint patties. "Allison is supposed to be cutting back on sugar."

"I wonder if she eats licorice whips and rainbow sherbet in the middle of the night." James smiled at her, holding his breath, sure he'd gone too far.

Sara laughed. And James exhaled. She shook her head. "I still can't look at red licorice without feeling pregnant."

"But your red tongue was so cute." He winked at her then wished he hadn't. As jittery as a boy with his first crush, he was second-guessing every word. *Lord, guard my mouth.* Too scared to wait for her reaction, he turned and dipped the paint roller in the tray.

"A person who can eat twenty-six hot dogs has no room to laugh at pregnant cravings."

"Touché." James laughed and looked at her over his shoulder. He'd come in far behind the winner at The Midwest Hot Dog Eating Contest at Mall of America. He shook his head in mock sadness. "I trained so hard for that competition, and my wife didn't even stick around until

I finished." Four months pregnant with Zoe, she'd run from the contest and left her lunch in the ladies' room.

Sara waved her hand as if pretending to slap him. "Can we get to work instead of talking about foods that make me sick?"

"Okay." He hated to stop the easy banter, but he needed to before he said something to burst the bubble that surrounded this moment. "Where should I start?"

She pointed. "Let's start in the corner to the left of the door and go clockwise."

That's my Sara. She'd always had a system for everything. Including him.

&

They worked in silence. Possibilities did a dangerous dance in Sara's head. She couldn't explain her change in attitude. Reece's words had suddenly whispered to her: *Give James a chance. He's not the same guy who walked out on you. He loves you, Sara.*

James had asked to talk. What was the worst that could happen if she agreed to listen? She'd get defensive when he accused her of not being the kind of wife he needed? *Been there.* She'd find out that the most important thing to James was James? *Done that.* There was no way she'd let him spend time with the girls. She couldn't take the chance of Zoe finding out who he was and then having to say good-bye again. But as for herself, he couldn't hurt her any more than he already had. She really had nothing to lose.

She climbed three steps up the ladder and looked down at him. Muscles stood out on his forearm as he pushed the roller up the wall. His hair curled behind his ear. She swallowed hard. "Brock said you're not with a band anymore."

"Never really was, to be honest." He looked up at her and gave a brief shrug. "It never got off the ground. Maybe my heart just wasn't in it." He turned back to his painting. "I've been playing at a little tavern near King's College. It's not a rowdy place, kind of highbrow and quiet with law and med students discussing stuff that's way beyond me. Still, I don't like working in a bar. I'm starting a new job at a supper club on New Year's Eve. They've got an eighty-year-old mahogany Kemble I can't wait to get my fingers on." His right hand played piano keys in the air.

Music. Her old competition. James may have changed, but that part of him never would. "You. . .wanted to tell me something."

Eyes the color of summer sky stared up at her. He nodded and turned back to the wall, used up the paint in his roller, and refilled it. James, the self-assured musician, was afraid to talk to her.

"Can I ask you something?" he asked.

"I. . .suppose."

"Are you and Reece together?"

"Is that why you're here? To check up on me?" Her questions came out harsher than she intended. Considering what Connie had probably told him, she shouldn't be surprised that he asked.

His fingers tightened around the handle. "Partly. If you're serious about him, I guess there's no point—"

"I'm not." She couldn't explain her need to rescue him before he finished the sentence. "There's nothing going on, never was. He came to talk to me about Jesus, and he hugged me good-bye. That's what your mother saw."

James exhaled through his nose. "Okay." His shoulders lowered.

"Is that it? What you wanted to talk about?"

"No." He set the roller in the pan. "You know—probably better than anyone—that my mother raised me to believe that I could do anything I set my mind to." He shrugged, looking embarrassed.

Sara turned around and sat on the ladder step, facing him.

"I was barely old enough to reach the piano when she told me I was gifted and I should never let anything or anyone get in my way because I was going to be famous someday."

Sara nodded. She knew all this. She was the "someone" who had gotten in his way.

James stepped back and perched on the back of the couch. "I'll save my list of lame excuses for another time, but the thing is. . .I actually believed her. I thought I was destined for something huge." He blinked several times. "You and the girls were interfering with my destiny."

Did he remember that he'd once screamed those same words at her? This time, though, they brought a different kind of hurt. This time, she wanted to cup his face between her hands.

"The real world smacked me hard. I should have learned that the first time I ran away. The first shock was when Reece ditched me because I left you. In my deluded state of grandeur, I thought he'd support my destiny." James shook his head. "I borrowed money from everybody I could and got to London with nothing but my inflated ego and my keyboard. Didn't have a penny or a plan, just that crazy dream of making it big in England where all my heroes started." Pain-filled eyes stared into her. "And. . .it was far enough from you to keep me from running back." He rubbed his hands on his jeans. "Anyway, the next year and a half I'd pretty much sum up as hungry and miserable. I washed dishes and swept floors and played in smoky little dives. That's where I was back in June when Reece showed up."

Sara's neck muscles tensed. She didn't like where this was going. "And talked you into becoming a Christian."

James smiled. "Yeah. . .but not quite like that. He didn't preach at me. I knew there was something different about him in the first two minutes. The amazing thing was that even a few months before that I wouldn't have been willing to listen. You know the story of the prodigal son, right?"

Sara gave a stiff nod. Her pulse hammered in her ears. She'd been "witnessed" to more times than she could count. Every

Sanctuary volunteer had their defeat-to-victory "testimony." Some of them she could repeat verbatim.

"Just the week before, I'd taken stale bread from an Italian restaurant's Dumpster. Just like a scene out of *Oliver Twist*. So when Reece said that God had told him to find me and—"

"Stop." She held up her hand. "I'm happy for you that you found God. But I'm not there. I'm not desperate. I'm doing just fine without it, James."

eight

After Mattie left on Thursday night, Sara scanned the weekly Dollar Saver flyer, highlight marker in hand. The plywood factory where Raquel worked had a third shift opening. The Sage Stoppe, where Sara had once worked as an assistant cook, was looking for someone to bus tables. Brock was right—this close to Christmas was not a good time to look for a job. College kids were home, and businesses had already hired their holiday help.

She folded the paper and tossed it onto the end table. It fell off, landing on a stack of magazines. On top of the stack sat "the book."

She stretched toward the table and picked it up. Curiosity had kept her from throwing it out. Just what was the recipe for a godly wife? A cup of submission, a spoonful of "Yes, dear"? Throw in a healthy dose of "Your slightest wish is my command"? She stared at the cozy couple on the front cover, wanting to make fun of their air-brushed happiness. But she couldn't. The woman had on a one-piece apron like the kind Sara wore at work. Her husband's muscled arms wrapped around her from behind. . .and made it hard for Sara to breathe.

"Riley J. Schmidt" was the name splashed in black across the white apron. "Figures. Bet his little wife was thrilled when he wrote it." Yawning, she opened the back cover—and blinked twice. Riley Schmidt had shoulder-length blond hair and wore a diamond pendant with matching earrings. She looked neither male nor nineteenth century-ish.

Finding the table of contents, Sara scanned the chapter titles. "Stir in Laughter," "Spice It Up," "Study the Cookbook—Together," and "Are You Ready for the Banquet?" She let the pages flip until they fell open near the middle of the book, to a chapter called "Making the Most of Leftovers." She read the first paragraph her eyes focused on.

> *If your man is married to his job and you feel, at best, like the mistress, you have to ask yourself one tough question: Why? What's driving your man? The need for approval or respect? A real need to generate more income? Are the requirements of his job beyond his control? Is it possible that God is asking you to graciously sacrifice time with your husband for a greater good? Or. . .the hardest question of all. . .is there a reason why your husband would rather be on the job than at home?*

Sara slammed the book shut. She'd picked a random paragraph and found just what she'd expected—the guilt trip. "It all comes back to the little woman's fault, doesn't it?" She sent the book sailing across the floor for the second time.

The subservient Riley Schmidt had the right question— *why?* She just didn't ask it right. *Why* would a man with two precious daughters and a beautiful home give it all up for a pie-in-the-sky career? Sara closed her eyes and pictured the two-bedroom townhouse, the furniture she'd reupholstered, the color scheme she'd carried throughout the house. She remembered the paint colors. . .Pumpkin Pie, Eggnog, Plum Passion, Wild Sage, Bittersweet.

It hadn't been easy. They'd each held down two jobs, but they'd worked it out so that one of them was always home. There hadn't been money for extras like eating out or movies, but the sacrifices had been worth it. She'd made a home they could all be proud of, and with each paycheck, their Stillwater Inn fund grew.

In the soft glow of the dwarf Christmas tree, she scanned the shabby room and the ragged furniture. She hadn't done much with it. They were, after all, just passing through on their way to Stillwater. The thought eased her tension. She rested her head on the couch pillow and closed her eyes. The colors of her future home floated through her head. Dusky Violet, Antique Pearl, Victorian Mauve...

❧

A loud knock woke her. Disoriented, Sara stared at the Christmas tree. It was still dark. She had no idea what time it was.

"Sara!" The sound of keys jangling accompanied Raquel's yell.

Shivering and heart pounding, Sara stumbled to the door. She opened it and stared at Raquel, in jacket and gloves, her hair a mess and her heavy makeup smeared. "What's wrong?"

"I have to take Allison to the hospital. I'm afraid she might be losing the baby."

"What can I do?"

Raquel shook her head, fear evident in her eyes. "Just pray and call Mattie. And we won't be able to watch the girls today. I'm sorry."

Sara nodded. "Call me at work when you know something." She walked back into the apartment and turned on the light. The wrought iron clock above the television said it was just after five. She needed to leave by six this morning. Two couples were arriving before noon, and Sara had left too many things undone when Bessie had sent her home early last week because they both "needed time alone." Not that she'd gotten a moment of alone time on Sunday.

Grabbing the key to Raquel's apartment, she ran across the hall. It took several minutes to find the phone on the counter in the bathroom. She dialed Mattie's number. Eldon answered. Mattie was out on a rescue call. Eldon promised to pray for Allison and have Mattie call when she got home.

Sara pushed the OFF button. The women who lived upstairs both worked days, and she couldn't think of anyone else. This had never been a problem when Connie watched the girls. If she'd been busy, either Grandpa Neil or Brock was there. *Brock*. His days off varied each week. There was a chance. She dialed his cell phone number. There was no way she was going to call the house phone.

The phone rang three times before she heard Brock's groggy voice. "Sara?"

"Hey. Sorry to wake you. Allison's having some problems and—"

"With the baby?" Brock sounded suddenly wide-awake.

"Yeah. Raquel just took her to the emergency room."

"Whoa. Okay, I'm on my way. If you talk to her, tell her I'll be there in fifteen minutes, maybe less. Bye."

Sara stared at the phone, her tired mind trying to process what had just happened and what to do next. If she couldn't get to Tippet House this morning, Bessie would try to do her own work plus Sara's. Bessie simply didn't have the strength or energy for that. There was really only one option, and it involved admitting to Connie that she couldn't handle things on her own. Before second thoughts could take over, Sara pressed the numbers. For the first time ever, she hoped the voice she heard would be her mother-in-law's.

It wasn't.

James's sleep-heavy voice took hers away. Memories flashed like fireworks, and she had to brace herself on the bathroom counter.

"This. . .is Sara."

"Good morning."

Sara closed her eyes. His words slid over her like a caress.

"Sara? Is everything all right?"

Nothing is all right. You should be whispering good morning in my ear. We should be together and happy and— She turned on the cold water, held her hand beneath it, and splashed her face. "I'm sorry to wake you. I need to talk to your mother."

"She's not here. She and Dad went to pick up Granny. Is something wrong?"

The walls of the tiny bathroom pushed in on her. She opened her mouth but couldn't get enough air. Almost running, she strode through the apartment and out into the entryway.

"Sara? Are you still there?"

She opened the front door. The shock of cold helped her find her voice. "Yes." She hadn't realized until that moment that she was crying.

"Tell me what's wrong."

"I need—" A thousand things filled the blank. She pressed her fist against her forehead and took a long, slow breath. "I just need to find a sitter for the girls."

"When? I can watch them."

No. She couldn't let that happen. Not to Zoe and Sadie or to her. But they'd be safe with him, wouldn't they? And she could find someone else for tomorrow. Maybe it would only be for an hour or two. Maybe Mattie would get home. . . . "Now. I'm sorry. I have to leave for work, and my sitter can't—"

"I'll get there as fast as I can."

❧

Back in her own bathroom, Sara stared in the mirror while she waited for the water in the shower to get hot. Her face was pasty white. Sweat dotted her upper lip, and her mouth watered with a sour taste. When she was a little girl, her mother had told her to breathe with her mouth open if she thought she was going to throw up. After several breaths, the churning in her stomach calmed to merely rolling. She stepped into the shower and closed the lined eyelet lace curtain. It was the only thing she'd bought new since the tornado and would be the only furnishing she'd take with her to Stillwater Inn— her castle. Her castle that didn't need a prince.

But James was playing the part well. She turned the water temperature up until the spray hit her face like hot needles. He'd be in the car by now, probably speeding to get there. . . for her.

She should have said no. After this, he'd think he could come over anytime. The girls would get attached, and he was going back to London in fourteen days. It startled her that she knew that. Was something in her subconscious counting the days? She finished her shower and got out, racking her brain for any alternative. She ran a brush through her hair then wound it in a towel. After slipping into jeans and a bright green sweater with jingle bells stitched to the front, she flew back to the bathroom. With one hand she held the blow dryer, with the other she put on mascara and lipstick, something she didn't usually do. This morning she simply needed the added confidence.

ಶಿ

The door was ajar. Her boots and jacket were on. The fuzzy pink puff ball attached to her Tippet House keys dangled from the canvas bag that waited by the door. The list of instructions and emergency numbers were taped to the fridge. When James walked in, everything was ready but her nervous system. He wore a snug-fitting gray thermal shirt beneath the leather jacket. A small duffel bag was slung over his shoulder. A day-old beard darkened the contours of his face. Finger tracks showed in his hair. Long ago she'd left lines in that soft brown hair. . .

Sara called on every ounce of will she could muster. "I'm so sorry I had to ask you—"

"You didn't. I volunteered, remember?"

The man had an infuriating way of interrupting her and messing with her train of thought. "Thank you. There's a note on the fridge with everything you need to know. Breakfast is cereal, soup for lunch. Suppers are in the freezer, all labeled. You just need to microwave them."

He smiled, the same grin that had once put the sun in her sky. "I have friends with kids. I'll figure it out."

"They have a bedtime routine. . .if you're still here then. My work number is next to the phone on the table. Call me anytime. I'm hoping to find someone to watch them, so maybe you'll only have to be here a little while."

"I brought clothes. I don't mind staying the whole time."

A thought hit like a fist. He was too tall for the couch. Would he sleep in her bed? "I already left a message for someone. I'm sure she can come over. . . ."

Appearing resigned, he nodded. "Will they be scared when they wake up and find me here?"

"I don't think so. Just tell Zoe you came to finish *Goodnight Moon*."

"Would you mind if I took them sledding?"

Sledding. Zoe would be talking about it for weeks. If Sara said no, it would be for herself, not the girls. "I. . .suppose. You'll need their car seats."

James reached in his jacket pocket and pulled out a set of keys. "Let's just trade cars."

Her head was starting to hurt. If she took the keys, she'd be committing to letting him stay until Sunday. She stared at the gold *C* on Connie's key chain. The sour taste rose again in her throat. She opened her mouth and breathed. "O. . .kay."

"They'll be fine. We'll have fun."

She nodded. That was one of her biggest fears. She walked past him and picked up her bag.

"I didn't tell them who I was."

She stood statue-still, her back to him. "I know." *Thank you*. She faced him, feeling something close to a smile pull the corners of her mouth into a straight line.

James tossed his duffel bag onto the chair and took a step toward her.

Sara took a step back.

"Sara. . . I know it's killing you to accept help from me. You don't have to prove to me that you're a competent mom, that you don't need my help. I know that." His fingertips touched her sleeve. "I'm not doing this for you, okay? I'm doing this because I need to connect with my kids. Maybe you and I are over. I don't blame you for hating me. But the girls need a father, and unless there's someone else in the picture, I'm still it. I've screwed up big-time, but please. . .give me a chance to make it up to them. I won't tell them who I am until you're ready. Just give me a chance to be a dad."

Tears sprang to her eyes, and no amount of willpower would stop them. James stepped toward her, and this time she didn't back away.

His arms slid lightly around her. His breath brushed her cheek. "I won't ask you for anything more than that."

nine

James walked slowly through the quiet apartment. It was hard to imagine Sara living in this colorless space. He stopped at the girls' room and leaned on the doorjamb, staring at his sleeping daughters. Blond hair splayed across pink pillowcases; stuffed animals were snuggled in their arms. This room was the only place that showed any sign of Sara's creative touches. On one wall she'd painted a mural. Two little girls with jeweled crowns stood in front of a white house with green shutters and a wide front porch. Rocking chairs sat in a row behind carved spindles.

So Sara hadn't given up her dream even after all she'd gone through. Most likely that's all it was now—nothing but a dream.

James knew the place well. They'd spent their honeymoon, brief as it was, in this place Sara had dubbed "Stillwater Castle." Over breakfast on their last morning, Sara had told the owners that it was her dream to own a bed-and-breakfast. James remembered the rest of the conversation as if it had taken place yesterday.

"Come back in five years, and we'll sell it to you." Ingrid Torsten had smiled at her tall, Viking-looking husband.

Erik Torsten winked at his wife, and his huge hand clamped on James's shoulder. "We're planning our retirement. This place is kind of like our baby, you know? Don't want just anyone handling it. But we like you two. You start putting your pennies in a cookie jar, and we'll stay in touch."

It was all Sara had talked about on the way to their first night in the townhouse they'd just rented with the money she'd earned for tuition. "We can do it if we work really hard,

69

can't we, James?" Just thinking about it now brought back the same gut-tightening fear. Her cheeks had flushed pink as she stared at him. "Promise?"

He couldn't say no to those amazing green eyes. In spite of the knot in his belly, he'd grabbed her hand and kissed it. "Promise."

❧

He was sitting on the couch, leafing through the book he'd sent Sara, when he heard the soft padding of little feet. In bright pink pajamas, Zoe walked toward him, her curls in a wild mess. Without a word, she handed him a sad-looking, furless stuffed dog, turned around, and walked out. Minutes later, he heard the toilet flush, the water run, and then she appeared again in the living room with *Goodnight Moon* under her arm. She crawled onto his lap and leaned against his chest.

James put his arms around her and opened the book, but it took several slow, controlled breaths until he trusted himself to talk. "Should I start at the beginning?"

Zoe's chubby fingers grabbed the stuffed dog's head and wiggled it up and down.

"Okay, the doggy says we start at the beginning."

"Misser Peabody. His name is Misser Peabody."

James put his thumb and forefinger on a threadbare paw. "Glad to meet you, Mister Peabody." He bent down to look in Zoe's eyes. "He looks like he's been loved a whole lot. His fur is rubbed off like the Velveteen Rabbit."

His daughter giggled. "That's just 'cause the ternado flew him round and round"—she circled the dog in the air—"and stuck him in a 'lectric wire, and a 'lectric company man went up on a ladder on a truck and rescued Misser Peabody, and he was even on TV, and so was I."

James took another slow breath. "Was the tornado scary?"

Blond curls bobbed against his shirt. "It was so, so loud you can't believe it! We hided in the washing machines building, and Mommy said the ternado couldn't get us there, but I cried, and Sadie screamed, and our house just went *squoosh!* like when you step on a bug."

Regret burned like acid. If he hadn't left, his wife and kids wouldn't have been living in a mobile home. "I'm glad that man saved Mister Peabody."

"Me, too."

A soft whimper came from the bedroom. James looked up to see a purple sleeve retreat behind the door.

"Sadie's awake. She's very shy. I'll go get her and tell her you're not a danger."

"What's a danger?"

"Bad people that you don't know that give candy to little children and tell them to get in their car." Zoe slid off his lap then turned to face him with a stern expression that was a carbon copy of her mother. "We don't talk to dangers. . .ever."

૨ఖ

Outside the window, snow sparkled in the sunlight. Dust cloth in hand, Sara stood by the bow window in the Tippet House parlor on Friday afternoon and tried to keep her mind on her to-do list.

"Why don't you invite James and the girls here?"

Bessie's soft words cut into Sara's meandering thoughts. She turned and smiled. Bessie appeared thinner and frailer than she had a week ago. "That's sweet of you. But—"

"No excuses. Our guests won't be back until after eight. There's a perfectly good sledding hill in back that's useless in a place that doesn't allow children. If it weren't too late, I'd rethink that policy." Her chin jutted forward.

Sara picked up the handblown glass cardinal perched on the grand piano and dusted beneath it. She waved her hand across the room filled with glassware and antiques. "One of the charms of this place is that it's *not* childproof. Your policies are just fine, Bessie."

"Still. . .there are things I'd do differently. We all would,

I suppose." She folded the hem of her apron between her fingers. "Call James. After all I've heard about him, I think I deserve to judge for myself what kind of man he is."

Running the dust cloth over the hinged door that covered the piano keys, Sara sighed. "I think you'd like James."

"You say that like it's a bad thing."

Staring at Bessie's gnarled fingers, Sara shook her head and lifted the lid, exposing the keys. "The two of you have a lot in common. You should hear him play. . . ."

"I'd like to." Bessie smoothed the lace doily that sat beneath a Tiffany lamp and an antique candlestick phone. "It's the musician in him that scares you, isn't it?"

"Scares me? I'm not afraid of him."

"No. But you're afraid of *it*—the music that pulses through his veins, the thing he needs to feel alive."

The protest stopped before it reached Sara's lips. Bessie's red-rimmed eyes focused on the open keyboard. She may have insight into James, but she was talking about herself. "You miss it, don't you?"

"It was like air to me." Her words were soft, maybe meant only for herself. "When it became too painful, Warren thought it would be easier for me if we sold the piano." She smiled at Sara then wiped her eyes. "I couldn't even entertain the thought. Once in a while I have to grit my teeth and plunk out a tune in spite of the pain. It refreshes the music in my head."

Sara touched the ivory keys, not sure what Bessie had said that had caused her throat to constrict. "I guess I never did understand it. Maybe I didn't really try."

"Musicians are strange folk." Bessie picked up the candlestick phone and handed it to Sara. "Maybe it's not too late to understand him."

"You're a conniver, Bessie." The phone wasn't functional, but it made the point. "If I do—and I'm not saying I will— he can't know anything about me losing my job, okay?"

"Okay. Sara, what I said about doing things differently. . . marriage is one of those things."

"But I thought. . ."

"I know, I know. You haven't heard me say anything but good. But I have a lot of regrets." Bessie walked over to an arrow-back chair with a needlepoint cushion and sat down. "I was very good at getting my way."

Sara pulled out the piano bench. "Is that a trait of all musicians?"

A reproving eyebrow raised in response.

"Sorry," Sara said. "I was pretty good at getting my way, too. What do you regret the most?"

"Not pursuing adoption. We were promised a child once, but it fell through. I couldn't face going through that again, so I got my way. . .and Warren suffered for it. He would have been a good father." Bessie rubbed her wedding ring against her apron then tilted her head slightly. "Learn from my regrets, Sara. Call James."

❧

"Don't crash us!" Snow-crusted mittens slapped over Zoe's eyes.

James laughed and tightened his grip on her. "Here we go! Give us a push, Mommy."

Sara's hands pressed against his back, and the sled flew down the forty-five-degree slope. Zoe squealed until they tumbled off at the bottom. Giggling and breathless, she scrambled to her knees and waved to Sara and Sadie. "Let's do it again."

"I think it's your mom and Sadie's turn to use the sled." He held his hand out to her. "Help me up."

Shaking snow off her mittens, she looked at him then narrowed her eyes. Her eyebrows bunched together above her freckled nose. "Are you my daddy?"

"What. . ." James swallowed hard. "What makes you ask that?"

"Grandpa Neil showed me pictures of my daddy. You look like him."

"Oh. . ." He stood and picked up the sled. "Want to race up the hill?"

"I'll win. I'm fastest." Zoe's boots dug into the packed snow, and she darted ahead of him. James took one step to her three but didn't even try to catch up with her. He felt like he'd just dodged a fastball.

Like her mother, Zoe talked with her hands. She was gesturing wildly to Sara when James reached the top of the hill. ". . .and we falled off, and my face got smooshed with snow!"

Sara's hair framed her face beneath a red knit cap. Her skin was pink from the cold, and her eyes sparkled as she laughed at Zoe. James set the sled down and held it while Sara sat on it with Sadie tucked securely between her legs. He put both hands on the back of the sled. "Ready? Okay, here you—"

"So *are* you my daddy?" Zoe stood with her hands on her hips, head cocked to one side.

James pulled back on the rigid purple plastic and locked eyes with Sara. Her lips pressed together, her eyes closed, and she shook her head. "What did you tell her?" she whispered.

"Nothing."

"Go down!" Sadie reached behind her head and patted Sara's face. "Go down!"

Sara nodded toward Zoe, her gaze still fixed on his. "Stall her."

James pushed, and the sled slipped away from him. He watched it careen down the hill, only too aware of the wide blue eyes waiting for an answer. "So. . .Mrs. Tippet said we can have hot chocolate when we're done. Have you had enough sledding?" Cautiously he turned his head toward Zoe and was relieved to see her clapping for the sledders who had stopped at the bottom of the hill. Maybe he wouldn't have to try stall tactics. How long could a four-year-old's attention span possibly be, anyway?

Zoe waved at Sara. "They didn't fall off like us. . .did they, Daddy?"

❧

Sara carried a thermos, four plastic mugs, and a bag of shortbread cookies out the back door and down the walkway to the gazebo. Her legs trembled. Maybe learning who James was wouldn't radically impact the girls. Sadie was too young, and Zoe didn't fully understand the definition of "father." She wasn't in school yet and didn't know many kids with fathers who lived at home with them.

No, the real problem was Sara's. How would the revelation impact the life she was trying to build for the three of them? With a smile she didn't feel, she walked up the gazebo steps and held out the treat to the threesome bundled under a blanket on the bench that circled the perimeter of the six-sided structure. "Who wants a winter picnic?"

"I do!" Three voices answered. One seemed to hold the same forced cheer Sara struggled to sustain.

Pouring hot chocolate and passing out cookies ate up the first five minutes. When she ran out of distractions, Sara looked at James and nodded. His smile was sympathetic—not the victorious look she'd expected. He turned his hand over in a gesture that said it was all up to her.

Clearing her throat, Sara pressed her gloves together. "I have a surprise for you, girls."

"Chalocolate?" Sadie smiled up at her with a cocoa mustache.

James laughed, and Sara matched it, staring at the lines that spoked away from his eyes. They hadn't been there two years ago, but she had to admit she liked them. She pulled her gaze away and back to the girls. "You've had enough chocolate for one day, sweet stuff." She leaned forward and waited for both sets of sky blue eyes to stare at her. "You know that James is a friend of Uncle Brock's, right?"

The girls nodded.

"Well, he's really more than just a friend. He's Uncle Brock's big brother." The news didn't seem to matter in the least to either of them. "And. . .James is also. . .your daddy."

Sara's pulse pounded. In spite of the cold, her shirt clung to her skin beneath her jacket.

Sadie smiled around a mouthful of shortbread. Zoe grinned and looked at James. "I told you so!"

A shiver started in the small of Sara's back. "But he lives far, far away across the ocean, so we won't get to see him very often."

James zeroed in on her eyes like a heat-seeking missile. "I could change that in a heartbeat. . .if I had a reason."

ten

"Soon it will be Christmas Day. . . ." As James sang, his fingers stroked the keys. He smiled at the four couples sitting on couches and cushions in front of the fireplace. Candlelight reflected off the polished black top of the baby grand, and the room smelled of cinnamon and pine.

Sara walked in with a silver carafe, and for a moment James forgot where he was in the song. Watching her move. . . The way she glided silently around the room, refilling cups and bending with a fluid motion to pass a tray of cookies, made it too difficult to concentrate on anything else. He looked away and caught Bessie Tippet's smirk. Now there was a woman with an agenda. . .and James was already beginning to love her for it.

The girls sat on a huge round pillow on the floor. Sadie, barely keeping her eyes open, appeared mesmerized by the fire, but Zoe craned her neck to watch James's hands. Partway through "The First Noel," she stood up and walked over to him. He kept playing as he slid over to make room for her to climb up beside him. She rested her fingers on the board in front of the keys. James finished the song, and his audience clapped. Over their thank-yous and murmurs of "Wonderful" and "Beautiful," he turned to Bessie. "Thank you so much for letting me play. This is an amazing instrument."

Bessie nodded and walked slowly toward him. "Thank *you*." She ran her hand along a curve in the black wood. A tender caress. "You have no idea what that meant to me, James. These old walls have sorely missed music." Bessie touched a tissue to her eyelashes. "What a gift you have." She folded her hands on the reflective top. "And it seems you've passed it on to your daughter."

Zoe touched the keys, not pressing down, just caressing them lightly with the tips of her fingers. James looked up and caught Sara staring at them. She'd learned something in the past two years—the art of hiding her feelings. He couldn't read the expression on her face, and the realization settled heavily against his chest. Looking down at Zoe, he pushed down on an ebony key. "Now you."

Wonder-filled eyes turned up to him. "Can I, Daddy?"

It was at least the tenth time she'd called him that. She'd found ways to insert it while asking him to pass something at supper, while he helped Sara and Bessie clean up the kitchen, and while he'd kept them quiet by drawing snowmen and Christmas trees so Sara could prepare the tray of goodies for the guests. "For a few minutes, and then we have to go home and put you two to bed. Just be gentle, and don't pound on the piano."

Blond curls jiggled. "I'll be very careful." Slowly she pecked one key at a time, first randomly then starting at middle C and moving to her left.

Goosebumps raised on James's arm. He remembered being just about Zoe's age, playing each note, trying to memorize the sound each key made. For a moment, his hand rested on her shoulder, then he stood and let her have the bench.

Several of the guests were heading up the stairs. Sara had left the room, but Bessie still leaned on the piano. "Don't give up on her."

James looked at the woman with the stern-looking face but compassionate eyes, then he touched the top of Zoe's head with his hand. "I won't. I think she's got the gift."

"She does." A soft smile created rows of concentric curves on Bessie's cheeks. "But I was talking about Sara. Be patient and listen to the things she's not saying." A gnarled hand touched his sleeve. "Let her stay mad while she's figuring out how to forgive you."

❧

Zoe had already kissed her good-bye and was dancing around outside in the glow of the porch light, but Sadie's arms wrapped around Sara's neck like a vise. Sara whispered in her ear. "Tomorrow you're going to get out the craft box and make Christmas ornaments with. . .James." After two years of pretending that he didn't exist, she couldn't easily make the shift to calling him Daddy. Sadie's face burrowed into her neck. Maybe inviting them to Tippet House hadn't been such a good idea. Once Sadie got into a clingy mood, nothing would change it. Sara looked at James. "This isn't going to be pretty."

James squatted down and put his mouth near Sadie's ear. "Hey, Sadie Lady, kiss Mommy good night, and you can walk on the sky all the way to the car."

Sadie giggled and raised her head. "Can I walk on the stars?"

"And the moon and the planets."

A wet kiss banged into Sara's cheek. Sadie reached out to James and jumped into his arms. Sara's chest felt cold.

"Watch, Mommy. I can walk upside down."

James flipped her over and held her by her knees. . .big hands, wrapped around skinny legs. Sadie's stocking hat fell off. Sara bent to get it, but James was lowering Sadie so she could pick it up herself. Giggling, Sadie jammed it back on her head. "Let's go!"

Sara folded her arms. "I only let them have two stories before bed."

James smiled, moving Sadie's legs back and forth like scissors. "I know. I read the rules on the fridge."

"And even if they're tired, they have to brush their teeth after all the sugar they had tonight."

"Will do."

"Sometimes chocolate gives Zoe nightmares."

A slow smile curved his lips. "I remember."

Sara stifled the "Oh. . ." that formed on her lips. At a year and a half, Zoe had only let her daddy comfort her after what they'd come to call her "Oreo Dreams."

"Well, I'd better get Skywalker home." Without warning, James leaned over the bottom of Sadie's boots and touched his lips to Sara's cheek. Instinctively she drew back. James pulled away, too. "I'm sorry, Sara. I don't know why. . ." He turned and opened the door wider with his foot. Turning back, he gave her a sad smile. "It just seemed so. . .natural."

❧

Something a hundred times larger and fiercer than butterflies played havoc with Sara's insides as she drove Connie's car home through heavy, blowing snow on Sunday. Anxious about the girls, she'd finished stripping beds and cleaning bathrooms in record time, but now that she was headed home half an hour early, she wasn't at all sure she was ready to face what waited there—James, laughing with her girls, playing sugar daddy to the children he'd deserted.

If the weather had looked better, she might have stopped at Mattie's. In the two on-and-off-again years that Mattie had been one of her mentors, they'd had innumerable conversations about how Sara should handle it if James showed up in Pine Bluff again. Yet, after all those hours, Sara was having a hard time recalling much of anything. Fragments of a talk on healthy anger and conflict resolution flitted across her consciousness like the snow that blew horizontally in front of her windshield. "Hold hands and look into each other's eyes" was one of the rules for fighting fair in marriage. Hot tears stung her eyes.

A bizarre thought shot at her from a blind spot. Maybe *she* should leave. Maybe, in reality, she was the one who was all wrong. Not James, not Connie, but Sara. She couldn't compete with either of them on the entertainment scale. James had always nagged her about loosening up and having fun. Well, maybe she'd just get out of the picture altogether and let them make every day a party. What would it hurt if her children lived like the boys of Pleasure Island in Pinocchio? Bedtimes and schedules were overrated. Kids didn't need sleep as long as they had fun! Her foot pressed harder on the accelerator; her gloves squeezed the steering wheel. It dawned on her that she was driving a Ford Escape. How fitting.

Squinting and leaning forward, she searched for the corner that couldn't be far ahead. Her hand was poised on the turn signal lever when the stop sign came into view. At the last second, she pushed the lever up instead of down, announcing to the lonely white countryside that she was not going home.

Not more than thirty feet into her northward flight, rational thinking took over—crazy thoughts banished by a vision of Sadie singing her Sunday night "Pizza-pudding" song. Stepping on the brake pedal, she cranked the wheel to the left. Antiskid brakes shuddered, but the tires couldn't find traction on the slick road. Around the wet snow collecting on the windshield wipers, Sara saw a road sign—way too close to the passenger side. She cranked harder, felt the back end swerve, heard the tires dig down to gravel, and her Escape thudded to a stop.

The sport utility vehicle sat at an angle, leaning toward the ditch but not in it. Shaking, heart thumping, Sara put the vehicle in PARK and wrapped her arms around the steering wheel, her forehead pressed against the hard plastic. She wasn't hurt, not physically, the car wasn't stuck or dented, but that didn't prevent the tears that dropped to her lap. It struck her that this was a point where someone like Mattie would pray. But Mattie was the kind of person God would listen to.

She straightened up and pushed the FOUR-WHEEL-DRIVE button, something she should have done when she pulled out of Bessie's driveway. All she wanted now was to get home, say good-bye to James as quickly as she could, and wrap her arms around her girls. The smell of their hair, the baby softness of their skin, like an elixir, had pulled her through much worse things than running her mother-in-law's car off the road. She swiped at the tears that blurred her vision and shifted into REVERSE. As she swiveled to look out the rear window, something on the middle seat caught her eye. A frayed black backpack. . .the same one James had slung over his shoulder on his way out the door two years ago. Sticking out of the pack was a corner of a book. Only the bottom of the spine was visible, just enough to show the author's name. Schmidt. As in Riley J.

James had his own copy of *Recipe for a Godly Wife*? And he'd brought it with him? He'd probably memorized it on the flight over, just waiting for the moment when Sara would fall to her knees and beg him to teach her how to become a sweet-talking, slipper-carrying, master-serving little woman. And just what else did he tote around in that ugly bag? Bibles? More fire-breathing tracts? Maybe he'd already bought the pearls and heels that would complete Sara's domestic goddess image. Teeth grinding, she put the car in PARK, unfastened her seat belt, and stretched over the back of the seat.

The pack was heavy enough to hold a case of Bibles. Hefting it onto the passenger seat, she opened the flap slowly, as if it might be filled with scorpions or tarantulas. Grabbing the book with thoughts of hurling it into the snow-filled ditch, she yanked it out then stopped and stared. It wasn't the same book. . .or the same author. This one was written by Caleb A. Schmidt. And the title was *Blueprint for a Godly Husband*.

A teaspoon of conviction mingled with curiosity as she opened to the table of contents and scanned the chapter titles. "Under Construction. . .Always." "Read the Specs." "Solid Footings."

Once again she let the book fall open. The pages she stared at were marked with notes and underlined sentences. As heavy snow plastered the side windows, Sara read out loud from a chapter called "Plan B. . .or Z": " 'The two-by-four is a quarter of an inch too short, the oven won't fit in the space you made for it. . .what's your first reaction? Let the hammer fly along with a toolbox full of expletives? That was the extent of my coping skills a few years back—on the job and across the kitchen table. Let me tell you, guys, it doesn't work. Then again, maybe you're the kind who screams 'I quit!' as the hammer sails through the plate glass. . .or your wife dissolves into tears. If that describes your MO, I have to ask: *How's that working for you?*'"

After the last sentence, which was underlined in ink, were penciled two words in all caps: "IT DIDN'T."

❧

The sight of Brock's car parked behind hers in front of the apartment peeled off several layers of tension. He was probably breaking Sanctuary rules once again, alone with Allison, who had been sent home with instructions not to lift or climb stairs. But Sara would borrow him for a few minutes, just long enough not to be alone with James. Her reasons changed with each swipe of the windshield wipers—because she was scared to death of falling into his arms, because she might say something she'd regret, because maybe now wasn't the time to tell him he couldn't just jump back into his role without paying penance or serving time for desertion.

She walked up the front walk and took a deep breath as she stepped onto the porch and opened the front door. Muffled laughter and a familiar smell met her in the foyer. Her stomach twisted as she opened the apartment door.

"Surprise!"

James, Brock, Allison, Zoe, and Sadie sat at the kitchen table. In front of them were two baked pizzas and six bowls of chocolate pudding.

With a strangled sob, Sara ran to the bedroom and slammed the door.

eleven

"Do something!" Brock shot daggers at James, as if Sara's meltdown was his fault.

Allison's accusing gaze zigzagged between the two men then parked on James. "What was that all about?"

"Daddy, why is Mommy crying?"

James closed his eyes and took a prayer breath. *Lord, help!* It had been too long since he'd tried to figure out what to say to a crying woman. From past experience, "I'm sorry" was usually the place to start. But what came next? With four expectant faces locked on his, he stood and walked on jelly legs to the bedroom.

The door was open several inches. Sara had certainly used enough force to shut it, but the latch hadn't caught. His hand formed a fist, and he raised it to knocking position then froze. In the three days he'd been in the apartment, he hadn't set one foot on the other side of this door. Though the couch was too short and too lumpy, it was a neutral zone for thoughts.

In the fear-filled silence, he heard her crying. His hand lowered to his side. Maybe she needed time. Maybe *he* needed time. Time to prepare for launched pillows and lacerating words. A line from the book he'd read for the third time on the plane came to mind. *Let her get it out.* The advice dovetailed perfectly with Bessie's counsel. *Let her stay mad while she's figuring out how to forgive you.*

When he was little, his father had bought him a blow-up clown with a weighted bottom. A punch to the big red nose would send it to the floor, but the stubborn thing would always pop back up again. He could be Bop the Clown for her, rebounding after every blow. . .at least for a while. Without knocking, he opened the door and stepped over the stocking cap and boots she'd most likely fired at the wall.

Still in her jacket, Sara lay on the bed. The face that turned toward him didn't much resemble the funny little blond he'd fallen for five years earlier. Her hair was electrified from tearing the hat off. Her nose was Bop the Clown red. Wild, puffy eyes narrowed to smoldering holes. "Get out."

"Sara. . ." He took a step forward. "Sara, what did I do?" He suddenly realized how large a door that question would open. "What did I do. . .just now? What's wrong?"

Her head lifted from the pillow. "What did you do? You ruined ev–ry–thing, that's what you did! You made pizza and pudding with *my* girls!"

A smile threatened to move his lips from their tight hold. This is where he'd gone wrong way too many times. He had to take her seriously—even when she was overreacting, even when she looked so adorable with her face all scrunched and angry. He'd found out the hard way that saying "You're so cute when you're mad" wasn't the way to disarm the bomb. This one had to be disassembled wire by wire. And to do that, he had to see pizza and pudding through Sara's eyes.

"I'm sorry." Man, this wasn't easy. Sorry for leaving her, yes. Sorry for being an insensitive, self-absorbed idiot, yes. But sorry for baking a pizza? *Lord, show me. . . .* "That's your special thing to do with them, isn't it?"

"Yes." The word came out rough and gravelly.

"I should have realized that."

"Yes, you should have." She smashed her face into the pillow.

"I'm sorry." Enough, already! He was sorry. Brock had told him about the Sunday tradition; he should have realized that having supper ready for her when she walked in the door wasn't a help. But there were just so many times a guy could use those two words without feeling like a total slug. He needed to save them for the really vital things. "Sara? Can we talk?" Where had he heard that before?

"Talk? Sure." She leaned on one elbow. "Let's talk about how I had to quit my jobs and get out of *our* lease and move into subsidized housing. Or maybe you want to know what it feels like to apply for food stamps and medical assistance. Or how about all the choice little names I've thought up for you in the past two years?" She laughed, cold and biting. "Do you really want to hear what I have to say, James?"

He took a deep breath, another step, then made a move that was certain to hurt him in one way or another. He sat on the edge of the bed. "Yes."

Sara sat up, clawed at the buttons of her jacket, and ripped it off, hurling it at the floor. She drew her knees to her chest like a protective fortress. His one-word answer seemed to have created a lull before the storm. Raw pain, more than anger, blazed in her eyes.

"Do you have even the slightest idea what you put me through?"

"No." James held her gaze. He knew he needed to hear her out without defending himself, but he wasn't going to cower from her. Beyond the shadow of a doubt, he knew that his sins against her had been paid in full. It had taken a lot of late-night talks with a small group of God-honoring men and hours on his face before God to bring him to the point of accepting that he no longer needed to be punished for what he'd repented of. He did, however, need to face the consequences like a man of integrity. *A soft answer overcomes wrath.* "I can't imagine."

Sara turned to face the wall, her knuckles pressed against her mouth. A silent sob shook her shoulders, and James commanded his arms not to reach out. "I'm listening."

Red eyes blazed. Her fist lowered. "You. . .can't. . .do. . . this." Her words snapped out a staccato beat.

"Do what?" Try as he might, he didn't have the sixth sense

she'd always wanted from him.

"You can't just walk back in acting like two years was nothing. You can't use the Jesus card on me, James. I'm not that stupid. You can't tell me that in six months you've become this—this perfect, sensitive guy who's suddenly going to be an attentive, responsible father. It doesn't work that way. You forget. . .I know you. I know that the only thing that really matters to James Lewis is James Lewis."

Bam. Hit the floor. Get back up. *Lord God, I can't do this.* James rubbed his hand across his eyes. "I'm a work in progress, Sara. I'm a million miles from perfect, but I am different." He hammered his defensiveness back down where it belonged.

"For how long? Your brother went through a Christian phase, too. Remember? It lasted until Caitlyn Douglas died of leukemia after all her friends had prayed around the clock for weeks. What's going to turn you away, James? Do you honestly think I'd let you move back in like old times and just sit around and wait and pretend that everything's wonderful until something gets too hard for you again and off you go to Canada or England or Timbuktu?"

James dug his fingers into the dark blue bedspread. "I'm not asking to move in. I'm just asking for a little patience, Sara. I don't expect you to believe I've changed just because I say so. But the only way I can prove it to you is if we spend some time together and—"

"And you worm your way into my girls' hearts? No! I can't let you do that." She pointed to the door. "Just get out, James. Go back to your music and your roadies and quit pretending to be something you're not."

James released the fabric balled in his hands and stood up. "This isn't about the girls and you know it. This is about you. And if you ever decide to be mature enough to carry a conversation all the way through, maybe we'll actually get around to talking about your side of this. I didn't just walk out on a whim. I left because I finally caved in and agreed with you. I finally believed that you were right, that you could do it all better than me and better without me. My goals were getting in your way big-time, and running my life on top of yours and the girls' was just a bit too much of a strain on you, wasn't it? So I finally decided to just get out of your way." He turned, took two steps toward the door, and looked back. "You win, Sara."

❧

The door slammed and ricocheted off the loose frame. Sara stared as it wobbled to a stop halfway open. So it hadn't taken long at all for him to do exactly what she'd predicted. He'd walked out on her once again.

It shouldn't bother her. With all the scar tissue left from the first two times, her sense of pain should be calloused over. So why did it hurt to breathe? She heard the apartment door open and close. Her next breath wasn't quite so tight. She massaged the shoulder muscles that tension had turned to steel. He was gone now. Life would return to normal. . . except for the fact that she didn't have a job, and if she did get one, she didn't have a full-time sitter.

Her feet had just hit the floor when Allison stuck her head in the room. "Um. . .we're gonna take the girls over to my place. You can come get 'em whenever." She pulled her head back out.

"Allison! Wait!"

"Yeah?" The girl looked annoyed.

"Did they have time to eat?"

"We're gonna take a pizza with us. Give you time to. . .you know. . .chillax." She was gone again.

Chillax? Maybe the kid was right. Sara needed to regroup before she got the girls. Take a shower, grab a slice of pizza. Her eyes stung at the thought of pizza, but she didn't have the energy to get upset about that all over again. Her head hurt, her eyes burned. She flopped back on the bed.

James was gone. She said it to herself twice then again,

feeling the tension drain. But the ache in her chest was still there. Scenes from Saturday popped in her head unbidden. James and Zoe pulling the sled up the hill. James and Sadie huddled together in the gazebo. Guilt, like an old shoe molded to fit, slid around her.

This isn't about the girls and you know it. It's about you.

How dare he! Just like always, he'd twisted the facts and dumped it all back on her. He'd accused her of running his life. Well, somebody had to. If she'd left everything up to him, he'd have been gone every weekend, playing gigs from here to Liverpool.

If only he'd been able to tailor his ambitions to fit a family. She would have been fine with him doing an occasional concert on the road or even a regular Friday night job in the Cities. But right from the beginning, he'd been adamant about pursuing his fantasies of fame on the other side of the Atlantic. Why hadn't she walked away before letting her heart and brain get so enmeshed?

James had stayed in Pine Bluff when the rest of the group headed to Canada. "I'll stay until you and I are solid, Sara," he'd said.

"And then I'll go with you. I'll follow you to the ends of the earth, James."

An inaudible gasp slipped through Sara's lips. She sat up. Why had those words surfaced now? Was it a false memory, or had she really said it?

There'd only been a few weeks between the time he'd told her he loved her and the day she found out she was pregnant. She tried to put herself back in that place, tried to think like a starry-eyed girl in love with the guy who mesmerized her with his music and his compliments. Only five years had passed, but it seemed like forever. A dim memory came into focus. . .standing backstage at Pine Bluff's Veterans' Hall, watching the crowd as they sang along with the words her man had written. Imagining a stadium full of fans. . .

But all that changed with a pregnancy test.

Memories served no good purpose. Sara stood up, kicked her jacket out of the way, and walked toward the living room. She'd eat her pizza alone, take a long, hot shower, and—

Her mental list disintegrated.

James was not gone.

twelve

He stood in the middle of the living room, hands on his hips. Sara braced herself on the archway leading from the hall, feeling like a dog caught in a bear trap. He'd waited. . .just to finish her off. She stared, daring him to blame one more thing on her.

His hand reached toward his back pocket. "I came home for three reasons." He pulled out his wallet. "To see the girls—yesterday was a day I'll never forget. To have an open and honest dialogue with you—I guess until I get on the plane I'll still be hoping for that. And to give you this." One stride brought him just close enough to hand her a check. "I didn't want to mail it. I had a feeling you might not be opening my letters."

Sara looked down. She knew immediately what it was. It surpassed the running total in her head by 10 percent—two years of back child support plus interest. Brock had researched it and told her several times he'd sent James a bill on her behalf. She'd convinced herself she didn't want his money anyway, yet the imaginary tab continually multiplied in her head.

Reactions bubbled like a stew pot. Disbelief, relief, anger. This would pay off her credit card bill and tide them over for weeks if she didn't get a job right away. But she could have used it months ago after they'd lost everything. She thought of his story about digging bread out of a Dumpster. Was that all it was—a story? "Have you been saving this up all along?"

"No." James looked down at the floor. "If I'd made any money, I would have sent it."

"Then how. . . ?"

He gave a quick shrug. "I sold some equipment."

His voice was so quiet on the last two words she wasn't sure she'd heard him. He looked up but not at her, with eyes that spoke of hopelessness. Her insides twisted. "What did you sell?"

Again he shrugged. "Korgy." A thin-lipped smile accompanied the word.

Suddenly chilled, Sara hugged her arms to her waist. James had sold his keyboard—the 88-key Korg OASYS— the "synthesis studio" that did everything but make his coffee. She thought of the things she'd called the extravagant purchase—his baby, the other woman, the real love of his life. The thing that spawned their worst fight. Later she'd found out that his mother had paid for much of it. Armed with that new knowledge, Sara had been just as mad that James hadn't told her that up front.

He stuck his wallet back in his pocket. "She was getting old."

Tears stung her already sore eyes. James had sold his baby. For her.

Give James a chance. It was almost an audible voice in her head. She closed her eyes, opened them, and motioned toward the couch. "Sit down."

❧

Sara laid the check on the coffee table between them and sank to the edge of the chair. She rubbed the spot that throbbed above her right eye. What now? What were the rules for fighting fair?

She stared into crystal blue eyes and took a shaky breath. "Thank you. . .for the money. The timing is—"

"I know. I should have been sending something all along. I—"

"No." She offered him a hint of a smile. "Yes, you should have, but that's not what I was going to say. James, I lost my job. The bed-and-breakfast is closing."

James leaned forward. "I'm so sorry, Sara."

"Thank you." She ran her fingers along the frayed seam near the knee of her jeans. "But maybe the timing is. . .a God thing." She held her breath, hoping he wouldn't take her inch and turn it into a mile.

"Maybe it is."

She waited, but he didn't add anything more. Now what? She felt like she was holding her finger on a hand-grenade pin. One wrong word could blow away any chance of real communication.

She remembered another rule. *Speak the truth in love.*

She took a deep breath. Then another. "I'm scared."

James groaned. "Sara. . .so am I."

"I'm scared of trying and then finding out it's too late."

James nodded. "I know. But I'm scared to walk away without trying."

"I don't think we can talk without hurting each other."

"Then we need some help."

"I know a couple." Mattie and Eldon would probably consider it an honor to counsel them; that's just the way they were. "They've been married over thirty years, and they've gone through some bad times." She watched his expression, wondering why he seemed to hesitate. And then it dawned on her. "They're Christians. . .*real* Christians."

Blue eyes lit with a kind of glow Sara wasn't sure she'd ever seen. "Thank you," he said.

Was he thanking her or God? Maybe both. She needed to lay down some rules before she got cornered by three people with a God agenda. "The only way I'm going to agree with this is if you can promise not to push your religion on me anymore. No more books or tracts or guilt."

James sat back on the couch. The clock above the TV ticked louder than Sara had ever heard it. "I can promise not to push or give you tracts or books. . .but I won't promise to never talk about God."

In a strange way, Sara was satisfied with his answer. It was pretty much the same thing Mattie had said when Sara had asked her not to preach to her. She could accept James talking about what was important to him as long as he wasn't shoving it at her.

Leaning forward, James rested his elbows on his knees. "Do you think maybe you and I could do something fun together? Something unserious and unthreatening. . .just the two of us?"

Unthreatening. Looking at his eyes, at the dark hair splayed across his forehead, Sara knew that his very existence was a threat to the guard she'd put on her emotions. After today, after knowing the sacrifice he'd made for her, he'd still be a threat if. . .*when* he flew back to London. "Like what?"

"Like lutefisk."

"*What?*"

"Bessie slipped me two tickets to the lutefisk dinner at the Lutheran church on Friday."

"But I work on Friday."

"Not between six and eight. Boss's orders."

Sara hated the jelly-looking Norwegian delicacy, but a crowded codfish-smelling church basement would, like James had said, be an unserious environment. "I'm only eating the Swedish meatballs."

"Is that a yes?"

Her sore eyes and dull headache wouldn't let her forget what she'd been thinking about James just minutes earlier, yet his hopeful grin made her laugh. How in the world had her pendulum swung so far so fast? And was she crazy not to push it back? "Yes."

&

"Can I ask you a question?" Mattie spoke through the cinnamon-scented steam floating from her mug of tea.

Sara laughed. "Since when do you ask first?"

"Since we started talking about your marriage in the present tense."

"You can ask me anything. By now you know more about me than I do."

Mattie took a sip of tea, set down her cup, and pressed brownie crumbs with her fingertip. "Why didn't you stop wearing your wedding band when James left?"

A bite of still-warm brownie gave Sara a reason to stall. She chewed, on her dessert and on her answer. "People look on single moms differently. I don't want to be pitied or judged. . .or hit on."

"Is that all?"

"I suppose, deep down, I love the idea of marriage."

"Is that all?"

Sara wrapped her hands around her mug and sipped the hot chocolate spiked with coffee. "I know what you're trying to get me to say. I thought I'd given up, but maybe. . . I would have told you a month ago—I probably *did* tell you a month ago—that I never wanted to see his face again. If I was holding out hope that he'd come back and sweep me off my feet, it was buried deep in my subconscious."

Unbidden, her dream popped into her mind—the mistletoe in the white box and the kiss that followed—maybe her hopes weren't as buried as she thought.

"But he's changed enough that you're willing to get swept now?"

"Yes. Maybe." Sara set her mug down. "I'm afraid to believe it's genuine. Can being a Christian really change somebody that much?"

Laughter wasn't the answer she'd expected, but that's what she got. Mattie grinned at her. "What do you think I've been trying to tell you for the past two years? Change is what it's all about. There's an old saying in the church—God loves you just the way you are, but He loves you too much to leave you that way." Mattie reached across the table and touched Sara's arm. "I'm not sure what's holding you back. Either you feel that God doesn't care because of all the bad stuff that's happened to you, or you feel like you've done too much bad stuff for Him to *want* to care—"

"Or all of the above."

Mattie smiled. "All of the above is false. God loves you, Sara. It might not be evident right now, but He does. And when you finally surrender to that fact, you'll find out that people really can change that much. But God isn't a magic potion. You can't just say all the right words, and suddenly life is beautiful. It has to be a real commitment." She pointed at her chest. "In here. You don't have to have it all figured out, but you have to be sure in your heart that Jesus is who He says He is and that you want to give Him every part of you."

"James seems to think that if I just become a Christian, everything will be easy."

Again Mattie laughed. "Oh how I wish it were that simple. Marriage can be hard, and following Christ can be even harder. If James has been following Jesus for six months he knows that by now. One of the ways God changed me years ago was by making me realize that difficult doesn't mean bad. It just means difficult. I started looking at my marriage as a challenge instead of a hopeless mess. And years later, as an old married grandma, I can honestly say life is beautiful. Tough but beautiful." Her thumb wiggled the back of the ring on her hand. "Did you ever do the climbing wall at the Y?"

"Years ago."

"That's my marriage analogy. One precarious step at a time, you work your way to the top. Sometimes you feel stuck, lots of times you want to quit, but there's always another rock to grab or plant your foot on. And, for me, Jesus is my safety harness."

Sara laughed. "You sneak that little hook into every conversation, don't you?"

"That's who I am, Sara."

"I know." *Is that who I want to be?* "Maybe I need a safety harness."

❧

Kitty-corner from Sara, the man sitting next to James wore a sweatshirt with a picture of a Viking in a horned helmet on the front, and the words "Life is simple: Raid. Pillage. Burn. Repeat as needed." Suspenders in the red and blue of the Norwegian flag secured the pants of the potbellied man who brought their coffee. From a platform in the corner, a singer with a three-piece band sang "The Lefse Song" to the tune of "Camp Town Races." *"Norsky ladies sing dis song. . .Uff Da! Uff Da. Bake dat lefse all day long. . .all da Uff Da day."*

Sara looked down at the whitefish and boiled potatoes swimming in butter and cream sauce on her plate next to the meatballs slathered with brown gravy. She hadn't had the heart to tell the rotund little woman with the big red spoon that she couldn't stomach fish that had been dehydrated and soaked in lye. She took a bite of meatball. "These are great."

A huge forkful of fish hung from James's fork. "Try this. It's perfect. It only gets like jelly when they overcook it." He inched the fork closer. "Come on. You love fish."

Her eyes crossed as the fish drew closer. It would end up on her lap if she didn't open her mouth. One bite wouldn't kill her. She could hold down one bite. She opened her mouth and was shocked to find the fish flaky and not nearly as fishy tasting as she'd remembered from a childhood experience that had catapulted her to the bathroom. "Not bad. But even cardboard would be good with enough butter and gravy."

"Cardboard's not so bad with spaghetti sauce either."

She laughed and then remembered what he'd said about hunting for food behind an Italian restaurant. "Were you serious about stealing bread from a Dumpster?"

"Not the kind of thing I'd joke about."

He looked embarrassed. Clearly he hadn't expected her to delve any deeper into his comment. Sara picked up the piece of potato flatbread that was folded on her plate. She didn't want to open it up on the table the way she did at Christmas and Thanksgiving at the Lewises, but she'd watched James skillfully butter his in his hand. "Will you fix my lefse for me?"

"My pleasure." He laid the soft tortillalike bread across

one large hand, spread it with butter, sprinkled sugar over it, and rolled it tight. With a slight bow of his head, he handed her the cigar-shaped roll. "Always ready to help a damsel in distress." His face reddened on the last word, but he smiled. "I mean that. . .now."

I believe you. She couldn't say it out loud, but at least in this moment, she did believe.

❧

"These things are messy." James reached across the table and wiped a drop of whipped cream from Sara's chin. *Krumkake*—thin, crispy cones filled with whipped cream and lingonberries—was only one of the dessert offerings passed around by the teens of the Norway Lutheran Church youth group.

"That's what makes them good." Sara looked at him with a smile that momentarily banished five years of misunderstandings.

"But you make them better."

A half smile quickly slid behind Sara's napkin.

"You should open your own bakery." *Or bed-and-breakfast.* He hadn't asked her yet about the Stillwater Inn. Knowing he'd been the one to shipwreck her future made it a topic he really didn't want to approach. "Brock says you still bake a lot."

A wistful look drew her gaze to some distant place, but she smiled and nodded. "I bake. . .*baked*. . .at work, and Brock still gets his macaroons when he begs for them."

James took a drink of thick coffee from his Styrofoam cup. "I'm glad you and my little brother stayed friends."

"He's been a huge help, and he's so good with the girls." Her eyes came back to his, her expression slightly accusing, but James didn't sense anger.

This might have been a good place to insert another apology, but he couldn't form the words. "The mural in the girls' room is amazing." Where had that come from? Sara would see it for the subject shift it was, and it would probably lead to talk of Stillwater, a topic he'd narrowly avoided moments ago. He scanned the outside walls until he found his escape. "Think I'll hit the restroom before we leave." Crumpling his napkin, he stood and jockeyed around folding chairs and gray-haired Lutheran ladies until he found the men's room.

Cold water and a rough paper towel reddened his face but gave him the clarity to think. He'd been the one to suggest the guidelines for this date. Unserious and unthreatening. He was beginning to realize that was close to impossible. There were things that had to be talked about, and so many more reasons to say "I'm sorry." He walked back through the noisy room. The band leader was introducing a children's song called "Paul and His Chickens." It was time to leave.

Sara was on the same wavelength. She stood and grabbed her jacket before James had a chance to ask if she was ready. When they walked out the back door, Sara pointed down the hill toward Founders' Park, where pineapple-shaped lamps lined the west bank of the St. Croix. "Let's walk down by the river."

Only a sliver of moon hung over the water. Stars sprinkled the expanse above them like salt spilled across a black tablecloth. James watched the frozen vapor of their breath hover and then vanish as they walked along the sidewalk, close enough for hand holding. He stuck his gloved hands in his pockets. "Have you talked to the Torstens lately?" He kept his eyes on the poorly shoveled walk.

"Not for a few months. But I'm counting down the days."

He stopped. "You're still considering it? I thought that. . . when you had to quit your other job and—"

Her hand on his arm interrupted him. "They're offering me a land contract, no money down. Instead of retiring, they're moving to Southern California to help some relative run a vineyard, and they'll give me five years to come up with a down payment and get a conventional loan. Erik says I have a positive aura or something, and they want me to have it. To be honest, I think they feel sorry for me."

"Wow." *Thank You, Lord.* Of all the things that had haunted him in the past two years, Stillwater Inn was one of the worst.

"So that brings up a question, James." She pulled her hand away and tied her scarf tighter. "If we were to. . .work things out. . .could you handle that kind of life?"

Lord, help me here. An old familiar tightness gripped his throat—a caged feeling. Could he? So many conversations in his small group of men who were trying to let God put their lives back together had centered on sacrifice. Sacrifice and priorities and dying to self. "I won't make promises I can't keep, Sara."

❧

On Sunday afternoon Sara walked through the upstairs rooms of Tippet House for the last time. She took a moment in each bedroom doorway, as if saying good-bye to old friends. In the Penrose Room, which faced west, she pulled back the lace curtain. The storm that caused two cancellations last night had painted the countryside like a Christmas card. Rounded globs of snow decorated pine boughs, and cone-shaped mounds made swirled finials on fence posts. The sun had sunk to the treetops, like a bright orange ball speared on the tip of an arrow. Long shadows striped the snow-covered lawn, tinted pink by the setting sun.

At this time next year would she really be looking out the window of her own bed-and-breakfast? There were so many details yet to be addressed. She hadn't spoken to the Torstens in months. A larger question overshadowed the rest. If she found herself standing at a window of the Stillwater Inn, staring out at a winter sunset, would she be alone or with James?

He'd said he wouldn't make promises he couldn't keep. But would he make any promise at all?

Friday night, after James had dropped her off and ended

the night with a restrained hug, she'd stared at the ceiling in her third-floor garret for hours. Wrestling against hope had proved impossible, and once again she'd come to the conclusion that he couldn't hurt her any more than he already had. She couldn't possibly end up worse than before James walked back into her life. Their relationship would either begin to heal. . .or would end for good.

Now, two days later, as she waited for James to pull up the drive in his mother's car with their girls in the backseat, she knew beyond the shadow of a doubt that her middle-of-the-night conclusion had been totally false. If the fragile hope growing inside her shattered, this time she wouldn't bounce.

She let the lace slide back into place and picked up the basket of sheets at her feet. Rosy light patterned the wall and spilled into the hallway. She closed the door behind her and walked toward the stairs.

Halfway down, she saw Bessie sitting at the piano in tears. Sara set the basket on the floor, slid onto the bench, and put her arm around her. "I can't imagine how hard this is."

"What will I do in Arizona?" Bessie's shoulders shook with sobs. "This is all I've known for so long. . . ." She blew her nose, shook her head, and stared at Sara. "I need a purpose. I need to be needed, Sara."

"I'm sure you'll find things to do with your sister." Sara knew her words lacked conviction.

A soft huff preceded another blow of her nose. "My sister plays canasta and golf. That's her whole existence."

An idea began taking shape. "*I* need you, Bessie. I have a huge, huge favor to ask of you."

"What's that?"

"Would you use your tape recorder and make tapes for me of all your secrets? All the little touches that make this place so special—like the spices you boil on the stove at Christmas and what you put in the gift baskets for anniversaries and birthdays. I've taken a ton of notes, but you do so much behind the scenes during the week. It would really help."

Bessie sniffed then gave a weak smile. "I'll do that." She patted Sara's hand. "You know, if I hadn't taken out a second mortgage to pay for Warren's hospital bills, I'd just give this place to you." Her eyes filled again. "I hate to think of the house in anyone else's hands."

"Thank you. That means so much. And don't you go doing the guilt thing on me, you hear?"

As Bessie wiped at her tears, they heard snow crunching beneath tires on the drive. The engine stopped, and a car door slammed.

"That's James."

Bessie nodded toward the window. "Don't let that man get away, Sara."

"We're trying."

"You know, I'd stay in Minnesota if I could make a career out of saving marriages with church dinner tickets."

Sara laughed and touched her cheek to Bessie's. "You'll get all the credit if we work this out."

thirteen

While he waited for Sara to get her coat and gather her things, James picked up a shovel and cleared off the porch and the back steps, grateful for a way to channel nervous energy. In the car was a surprise he hadn't mentioned to Sara. Not a pleasant surprise.

The door opened just as he started shoveling the steps to the gazebo. Sara poked her head out. "All set."

James hugged Bessie and stacked bags and boxes, months of accumulated magazines, books, and toiletries, under each arm. As they stepped onto the porch, James took a long sideways glance at Sara, trying to gauge her mood.

"What are you staring at?" she asked.

My wife. "You. How are you doing?"

"Kind of sad." She fell in step behind him on the sidewalk.

Probably not in the mood for a shift from routine for the second Sunday in a row. "I bet." He slowed his steps and turned to face her. "Um..."

"Um *what?*" Sara stopped, peering over a pile of white bakery boxes filled with Tippet House gingerbread and shortbread cookies. "That look scares me. I already don't like what you're going to say."

"I know." James tried on a smile then cast it off. "My mother's in the car."

"Oh."

Whatever Sara was thinking, it wasn't on display. Was it good or bad that her thoughts no longer scrolled across her face like a teleprompter? "She needed groceries, and I had her car...."

There. For a split second, like a window opening and

103

slamming shut, he read the words in her head. *Groceries? On Sunday? She couldn't have sent you?* Or maybe he was just tuning in to his own thoughts, because Sara was actually smiling. Sort of.

They rounded the corner of the house in time to see his mother slip out of the backseat and into the front, leaving the back door open for Sara. *Could you be any more blatant, Mother?* From the first day he'd brought Sara home for dinner, he'd hated the crackling tension that spit like sparks whenever the two women were in close proximity.

Sara said hello first. His mother repeated the lifeless greeting. Sara slid into the car and transformed before his eyes. As he closed her door, hugs, kisses, and giggles filled the backseat. By the time he'd filled the trunk with Sara's bags and boxes and gotten in on the driver's side, the girls were singing "Mommy's home! Hurray for pizza! Mommy's home. . . ."

Beside him, his mother sat in chiseled stillness, staring at the gazebo as if it were a cinema screen. An outsider would have thought her deaf and mute. A dim light of understanding flickered in James's consciousness. His mother was jealous. All along he'd assumed the whole issue was that he'd married below her expectations. But maybe the problem was simply that he'd married.

Oddly, the realization made him smile. He put the car in gear and followed the drive that circled around the back of Tippet House. "Where to, Mom? Health food store's closed on Sunday."

Like a statue touched by a good fairy, his mother came to life. "Let's go out for dinner. My treat." Her hand patted his knee, and she turned toward the backseat. "Let's celebrate your last day, Sara."

Celebrate? "I'm not sure Sara's really feeling like a celebration."

"Well, she should be." His mother turned back to the front, then she opened her vanity mirror and adjusted it to get a view of Sara and the girls. "It's all about the way you perceive things. Dark thoughts are like toxins that poison your body and clog your spirit."

An image of a toilet plunger came to mind. Wouldn't jealousy count as a dark thought? James glanced in the rearview mirror at Sara's frozen expression. "How do you feel about going out for supper, Sara?"

Zoe nodded like a bobblehead doll. "Can we get pizza?"

The ceramic grapes hanging from his mother's ears swayed back and forth. "Absolutely not. The Sage Stoppe has pumpkin soup this week just for Christmas. Wouldn't that be a nice Sunday supper?"

Three faces fell in unison. James stifled his laugh. Sara looked beyond miserable. Little did she know she was about to witness firsthand the miracle of a life transformed. James stopped at the end of the driveway and fixed his gaze on the rearview mirror but spoke to his mother. "Mom, Sara has a tradition of pizza for Sunday night supper. If you'd like to treat, I'm sure they'd love it. Otherwise, let's pick up what you need at the store and take my girls home."

The blinking, incredulous stare from the woman with the amazing green eyes warmed him to his toes.

⊱

A girl could get used to this.

James kept his hand on the small of her back as the hostess ushered them to a rounded booth in the corner of Mama Gina's Pizza. The girls crawled to the middle of the bench seat, and Sara followed, which left room for one person next to her and one next to Zoe. Connie took a step toward Sara's side, but James set his hand on his mother's shoulder. "Why don't you sit next to Zoe, Mom?"

Without waiting for her answer, he sat down and scooted close enough to Sara that his leg touched hers. Could he feel that? Sara's sweater was suddenly heavy. How deliciously absurd to be so off-kilter over her own husband! *He's not the same man who walked out on you.* James had sold his keyboard and stood up to his mother. . .twice. Sara's doubts were dissolving like the snow on her boots.

As their waitress set down water glasses, the assistant manager walked up behind her. Sara had known Tom Wilkes since high school. "Hi, Sara." Tom nodded at James and Connie then turned back to her. "If you're still looking for a job, we've got a place for you as a server after the college help leaves. I know you applied to work in the kitchen, but we just don't have openings."

Waitressing was not what she wanted to do, but it was a job. And the look on Connie's face made her want to accept the offer on the spot. Connie knew people who came to Mama Gina's. What would they think if the wife of her gifted son was waiting tables? "What are the hours?"

"Weekends mostly. Four to twelve."

Not good hours for a babysitter. "I'll let you know in a couple days. Thanks, Tom."

Connie shook her head as Tom walked away. "James, don't you think Sara should go back to school and get her degree?"

His eyes on the menu, James chewed on the inside of his cheek. "I think Sara should do whatever Sara decides to do. She makes good decisions."

A girl could get used to this.

James ordered a large pizza—half deluxe, half ham and pineapple for "his girls." Connie ordered a salad, ate it with her eyes on the pizza, then picked at a leftover piece of deluxe, leaving it a barren crust. As she popped the last pepperoni slice into her mouth, she smiled at Sara, the kind of smile that triggered a silent *Uh-oh*. "We need to talk."

Uh-oh.

"I spoke to my spiritual director about you two." Though her words included James, her eyes didn't.

Sara prodded the corners of her mouth upward. "Oh? What, exactly, is a spiritual director?"

Connie appeared annoyed at Sara's ignorance. "Padma is my

life coach. She has amazing abilities. She can tell everything about a person just by their handwriting."

James rested his chin in his hand and arched his left brow. "Oh really?"

"Yes." Connie shot her son a glance and refocused on Sara. "I showed her your list of rules." Her mouth puckered on "rules" as if it left a bitter taste in her mouth.

A woman I've never met read my kids' bedtime and tooth-brushing rules and now knows all things about me? "Fascinating. What did she discover?"

"That you are a diamond."

Sara blinked. An affirmation from her mother-in-law?

"You retain your luster under adverse circumstances."

The statement was so unexpected that Sara didn't know how to respond.

Connie leaned forward. "However. . .diamonds also make excellent abrasives. A diamond person is often inflexible and can rub others the wrong way."

James's hand found Sara's—on her knee, where it was squeezing the life out of her napkin. Sara stretched her lips, baring her teeth. "How interesting."

"Isn't it? After Padma analyzed you, she looked at a letter from James." A full-out smile blazed on her son.

"And. . . ?" Sara and James asked the single-word question in unison.

"And. . .James is a star sapphire."

Of course he is. Sara choked her napkin. James tightened the pressure on her hand.

Connie laid her right hand on the table, all four fingers pointing at her star sapphire son. "Asterism. That's what they call the starlike phenomenon in a sapphire when it's exposed to a source of light."

Zoe and Sadie whispered and giggled over their Polly Pocket dolls. That was the only sound at the booth in the corner. James withdrew his hand, laced it with his other one on the table, and sat, in this prayerlike position, staring at his mother. Sara waited. The old James would have laughed nervously and suggested it was time to leave.

James cleared his throat. "Jesus said, 'I am the light of the world.' There isn't any star quality in me without His light, Mom."

"Oh, James. . ." A sound like a slowly deflating balloon leaked from Connie. "Embracing a religion can make you a happier person—though you'll soon find Christianity is far too restrictive—but it doesn't change your destiny. I knew you were a star from the moment I laid eyes on you."

As indignant as she felt at the moment, Sara couldn't resist humming the first few bars of a song from the Disney movie *Hercules.* . . . "*Shout it from the mountaintops. . .a star is born.* . . ."

James laughed. Connie flashed an annoyed look then manufactured an Oscar-winning look of despair. "Unfortunately, there's more."

"Brace yourself," James whispered, not loud enough to carry over the noise the girls were making. "What else, Mom?"

"I'm afraid. . ." Connie looked genuinely crestfallen. "I'm afraid that diamonds and sapphires are not spiritually compatible."

A warm hand slid back over Sara's. She glanced at James, tracing the strong line of his jaw with her eyes. Under the pressure of his touch, her anger melted into mere annoyance.

James shook his head. "So it's hopeless for us?"

"I'm afraid so."

He dropped his shoulders, hung his head, and gave a ridiculously exaggerated sigh. "What do you think we should do?"

Sara used her right hand to pull the napkin from her left then took great pains to wipe her mouth while covering her smile. How James was controlling his, she couldn't imagine.

"Diamonds do best with other diamonds."

"So Sara should be shopping around for another diamond?"

James twisted the plain silver band on Sara's ring finger.

"Don't make it sound so crass, James. You should both be searching for your soul mates."

Sara dropped her napkin on the table. "Don't you think we should be trying to work things out for the girls' sake?"

Connie looked up at the ceiling, as if she'd been about to roll her eyes and then decided against it. "Do you really want to spend the rest of your lives *working* at a marriage? What kind of a message does that send to your chil. . .to Sadie and Zoe?"

Picturing her father-in-law, parked in his favorite recliner, only the top of his balding head visible over the newspaper, Sara had her first-ever twinge of empathy for James's mother. Did she categorize the past twenty-five-plus years as simply "work"?

Was it her imagination, or did James lean just a fraction of an inch closer to her? He pulled his straw out of his empty soda glass, sucked on the end of it, then pointed it at his mother. "Nobody has a good marriage without work."

This was not the same man who walked out on her.

"It's good that you're talking now. Children need the security of parents who are at peace with each other, but just because you can be friends doesn't mean you should be married."

James tapped the end of his straw on the table. "Actually, Mom, I think that's exactly what it means. If Sara and I can manage to respect each other and communicate like we should have long ago, there's no way I want to settle for just being friends."

Sara's face warmed, and another song skipped through her mind—the one that said, "*I love you too much to ever start liking you.*" She felt the warmth of his leg against hers and looked over at the dark lashes that haloed sky blue eyes.

She couldn't imagine ever wanting to "just be friends" with this man.

fourteen

"What drew you to Sara the first time you met?" Eldon Jennet crossed his long legs and rested his arm along the back of the love seat. His fingertips played with the ends of his wife's hair. The seemingly subconscious gesture roused a sense of longing in James.

Fingering a loose thread on the Jennets' couch, James tried to dispel his fear of the unknown. He'd entered the comfortably worn living room feeling like he was walking into a dentist's office. In truth, he would have chosen a throbbing abscessed tooth over marriage counseling. But the first few minutes had passed without pain. What had first drawn him to Sara Martin? He glanced at Sara and smiled. "Whipped cream."

Eldon laughed. "Dare I ask?"

James told him about the pumpkin pie.

Mattie pointed at Sara. "That girl was sending signals."

"Oh yeah."

"Describe her." Eldon bent over and picked up a notebook and a pair of bifocals from the coffee table. "Tell us everything you remember about your first impressions."

This should be easy. He'd replayed that day so many times since he'd left. But with Sara sitting just inches away, it was awkward. He was about to use glowing superlatives to describe the woman he'd deserted. . .twice. "I noticed her eyes first. Her uniform was bright green, and her eyes just sparkled. . . like emeralds. The next thing that grabbed me was her voice." James smiled self-consciously. "I'd just heard a guy on the radio describing a woman's laugh as root beer fizzing over ice. That's what Sara Martin's laugh was like. It bubbled."

He'd never told Sara her laugh reminded him of root beer.

He slid a finger under the collar of his sweater, wishing he'd worn something else.

"Very poetic." Eldon raised his eyebrows. "What else?"

"Am I allowed to say I noticed her body?"

Mattie laughed. "You're allowed."

"Well, okay. . .I noticed. . .curves. Maybe I noticed that before her eyes." He laughed, fully aware that he sounded about fourteen. "And her hair. . .it kind of looked windblown, not stiff, you know?"

Eldon wrote something on the notebook. "What else?"

Was everything he said going to be recorded? Maybe Eldon planned on giving Sara a copy to remind her of the good stuff when they got to the inevitable bad. Or maybe it would be James who needed the reminder. "She asked questions— tons of questions, mostly about music and what kind of songs I wrote."

"And you liked that?"

"Of course. What guy wouldn't like a gorgeous woman wanting to know everything about him?" He took a quick, shy look at Sara, who was covering her mouth with her fingertips. "She fed my ego big-time."

꽃

"What else?" Eldon chewed on the end of his glasses.

Sara was getting used to that question. "I felt special. Our honeymoon was the first time I had his full, undivided attention."

Up to this point, Mattie and Eldon had steered them toward good memories. Sara hadn't known until tonight that they'd been trained as lay marriage counselors. They knew what they were doing. Mattie curled her feet beneath her. "What did James do, specifically, to make you feel special?"

Mattie's casual posture relaxed Sara. The tension that had started building when the spotlight turned from James to her began to ease. Her spine conformed once again to the back of the couch, and her breathing slowed. "He listened, and. . .he looked at me."

"That was unusual?"

"Yes. I mean, he was always looking at me, but while we were in Stillwater, he gave me eye contact. And. . ." She hadn't wanted to be the first one to bring up negatives. "I didn't have to share him with his music. For three whole days, it was just us."

Two feet away from her, she sensed James stiffen. He wasn't allowed to argue or voice an opinion during this part. This was Sara's turn to express herself without interruption.

Eldon scribbled something in his notebook and nodded. "What did you do, other than the obvious, on your honeymoon?" He winked at James, causing Mattie to roll her eyes.

Sara thought back to those three near-perfect days in Stillwater. How many times had James told her he loved her more than anything? How many times had he apologized for running when he found out she was pregnant and for thinking he could be happy without her? "We took walks, and we talked about the baby and how—" She reached for the coffee mug she'd set by her feet. The coffee was room temperature, but maybe it would coat the sudden rasp in her voice. "I remember James saying that he or she was going to be the luckiest kid in the world. . .because we were going to be the best parents ever."

❧

"Hi, Cal. Is Mom around?" Sara pulled flour, baking powder, and powdered sugar from the cupboard as she waited for her stepfather to find her mother. The hand that held the phone was clammy. She dug out measuring spoons and cups and two mixing bowls.

"Sara?" Her mother sounded breathless and worried.

"Hi, Mom. How are you?"

"What's wrong?"

"Nothing. I just wanted your Russian tea cake recipe."

The second hand jerked out four ticks. "I'll add minutes

to your calling card, honey. I'm fixing myself a cup of hot chocolate, and I'm settling in. You know that recipe backwards and forwards, so tell me why you really called. Is it James?"

Tears blurred the words on the back of the sugar sack. "Uh-huh."

"Are those good tears I hear or bad?"

"I don't. . .know." Sara threw the ring of plastic spoons at the bowl. "We met with Mattie and her husband for counseling tonight."

"How did it go?"

Again she wanted to say she didn't know. "We spent an hour talking about how we met and everything that we admire about each other and skirting around all the garbage."

"Seems like a good way to start."

"At the end they asked us if our relationship was worth fighting for."

"How did you answer?"

"James said yes. I said maybe." Sara stared at the ingredients that lined the counter like soldiers waiting for orders and shut off the kitchen light. Pulling a blanket off the back of the couch, she "settled in" by the Christmas tree.

"What would it take for you to say yes?" A whiff of impatience floated on her mother's voice. There were times they could be two adult women and times when Sara was locked in little-girl mode. Tonight she'd been hoping for a friend instead of a mother.

What would it take? "A guarantee."

Her mother laughed. "Buy a dishwasher, honey."

Sarcasm was not what she needed right now. "I can't take a chance on him leaving us again. If anyone should understand that it's you, Mom." She hadn't intended it to sound mean, just honest. Adult.

Four. . .five. . .six clock ticks. "I've come to the conclusion that we have so much more control over that than we want to think."

If this conversation was leading to guilt, Sara wanted no part of it. Her mother and Don Goode, Sara's biological father, had never married, never even lived together. They'd continued to "see each other" until Sara was a freshman in high school, when her father married one of the other women he'd been "seeing" for years. The news barely caused a ripple in Sara's life and surprisingly seemed to set her mother free to finally find a man who respected her. "Explain."

"One of the older ladies in my quilting circle summed it up perfectly: 'Even a lizard won't leave a sun-warmed rock.' If I'd been warmer, he might have stayed."

Laugh? Cry? Scream? Sara ricocheted among the three, landing on a sound that combined them all. "But he'd still be a lizard! And I don't want to be anybody's rock!"

Her mother laughed. "I'm just saying that it takes two."

"James left me, Mom. I didn't kick him out. Don wouldn't marry you. His choice—not yours."

A soft sigh. "You can't fix something if you can't admit it's broken."

Sara's fingernails raked a path in a champagne-colored throw pillow. "You're talking about me—not the marriage—aren't you?"

"You. . .and me. I couldn't have fixed your father, but I could have changed me. What was your part in James leaving, Sara?"

Fingernail tracks crisscrossed the pillow. "I didn't call to get a guilt trip."

"But you called for honesty."

She'd never gotten anything less from her mother. Still, she bristled against it. "Do you want to tell me what my part was?" Not too many years ago her sassy tone would have gotten her grounded.

"Do you want to hear it?"

Sara covered her legs with the blanket and lay down on the pillow that looked like a fresh-plowed field. "I'll listen."

"You clipped his wings, honey."

Her mother's words crunched into a fist, finding their

mark just below her sternum. Instead of a comeback, all she had were tears. "I have to go."

"Call me back when you have your own answer to the question. I don't care what time it is. Even if you're mad."

Sara closed the phone. Maybe she'd call back. Definitely she'd be mad.

≉

"Married men aren't supposed to have wings!"

Sara glared at her tear-reddened face in the bathroom mirror. Two inches of toothpaste squirted from the tube; some landed on her toothbrush, the rest in the sink. Once again, James was costing her money.

I didn't clip his wings, Mother. Sara watched the image in the mirror scrub at her teeth with the same rhythmic motion she washed the kitchen floor. She washed floors on Monday. James had hated her schedules. James wasn't a schedule person. He was a fly-by-the-seat-of-your-pants person.

Fly. . . What was her part in James leaving?

She spat in the sink, rinsed her mouth, rinsed the sink, dried the sink. . .a system for everything. When had that started? She'd always been organized, always liked things clean, but when had the craziness started? She stared at the toothpaste cap, and the answer materialized. When she couldn't control the rest of her life. When James was unpredictable, when she didn't understand the free spirit she was married to, when he had dreams that didn't match hers.

You're afraid of it—the music that pulses through his veins, the thing he needs to feel alive.

Maybe Bessie was right.

≉

Music woke Sara early. She'd set the radio alarm for six, giving her at least an hour and a half before the girls woke up. One way or another, by the end of this day, she would have a job.

Her hand groped for the snooze button before her eyes opened, but a voice stopped her.

"Top o' the mornin' to ye, Pine Bluffers! This is Nick Joplin opening December 23 with a song and a prayer. We're an hour and fifty minutes from sunrise, but it's already a beautiful morning because we're starting it with Jesus. Next song we're going to—"

Sara hit the SNOOZE button. The girls must have been playing with the radio knobs. Or James. He could have sneaked in and changed the station. The first time she'd started her car after he'd used it, some preacher had screamed at her in stereo about bringing her tithes to the storehouse. At least the volume on her clock radio had been low. She slipped back into a heavy sleep and woke nine minutes later with a heart-thumping start, to the deejay's absurdly cheery voice.

". . .love that song. Always makes me think of Psalm 139—'Search me, O God, and know my heart; test me and know my anxious thoughts. See if there is any offensive way in me, and lead me in the way everlasting.' I don't know about you, friend, but that's a hard one for me. I'm not too quick to ask God to point out the offensive stuff in me. But I have to wonder why David talked about anxious thoughts and offensive ways in practically the same breath. I'm thinking that maybe if we let the Lord search our hearts and dredge up the junk we need to pitch out, we won't be so anxious. Well, ponder that on your way to—"

Sara smacked the OFF button and sat up. Was God orchestrating some kind of conspiracy against her?

I'm praying that God won't leave you alone until you admit you need Him.

Mattie's prayer. Sara rubbed her eyes. Was that what this was all about? Was God using Bessie and her mother and James and the hyper guy on the radio to pester her until she caved in? Caved in to what?

Instinctively she knew the answer to her own question. Caved in to Him.

But what did that mean? What would that look like? Would

God really take away her anxiety, fix her marriage, protect her girls, find her a job? Or would He make her content without those things? She'd heard Mattie and her friends say things like "Give it all to Jesus" and "Leave it at the cross." One of Mattie's favorites was "Have to surrender that one." Mattie spoke of answered prayer the way Sara talked about gingerbread. Stir it up, pop it in the oven, and wait. Mattie expected answers—"His way, His time."

Sara didn't know where to begin or if she even wanted to. It wasn't that she didn't believe there was a God. Any doubt she'd ever had was erased the moment the nurse laid Zoe in her arms. The perfection of her rosebud mouth, the delicate curve of little fingers that Sara knew even then were destined to play a piano. . . Zoe was not a product of chance or evolution or pure biology.

Sara believed in a Creator. And she'd learned enough from Mattie and from the few times she'd picked up a Bible to be convinced that, as Mattie would say, Jesus was who He said He was. What she couldn't wrap her brain around was a song she'd learned from a neighbor when she was only four: "Jesus Loves Me." She could believe He existed, but why would He want anything to do with her?

Search me, O God, and know my heart. . . .

She clenched the edge of the blanket, drew her knees to her chest, and closed her eyes. "God, I don't know what You want from me," she whispered. "I'm tired. . .of doubting James. . .and You, but I don't know where to go from here."

Not even sure if her words constituted a prayer, Sara threw off the covers, got out of bed, and went in search of the phone. Unless that, too, had changed, there was one person she was pretty sure would be awake before the sun. She found the card in the silverware drawer and dialed the number.

"Minnesota Cabins. How can I help you?"

"Hi. This is Sara. I wanted to talk to you about that job offer, Reece."

fifteen

Two things were penciled on Sara's calendar for December 23. Shopping with James was first. It was her idea to use a little bit of the money James had given her to take the girls for lunch and Christmas shopping. The second thing on the calendar was counseling with Eldon and Mattie. Just looking at their names next to "7:00" in the neat white square hatched creepy-crawly things under her skin. The first session had uncovered good memories, but she had no illusions about tonight. To add to her stress, she'd agreed, in a weak moment, to let the girls spend the night with the Lewises. This time it wasn't just Connie who Sara was worried about. It was the man who would be dropping her off at her empty apartment sometime after ten o'clock tonight.

Keeping anxiety under lock and key all day would be a major undertaking.

By noon Sara had only one thing left on her to-do list. The girls were bathed and dressed and their backpacks filled with pajamas, stuffed animals, and gaudy tie-dyed Christmas dresses. The apartment was dusted and vacuumed, and her second round of Christmas cookies for Sanctuary residents was bagged and ready to go. She had only minutes until James would come by for her and the girls, but before she left, she needed to call Mama Gina's Pizza and tell Tom she wouldn't need the job.

Allison had come over around ten and taken the phone. "Zoe, run across the hall and get the phone."

"Me, too!" Sadie reached the door first, her dimpled hand poised on the handle, waiting for Sara's nod.

"Okay. Just come right back. . .and no treats. We're going out for lunch."

Minutes later they returned, shirts and faces peppered in Oreo crumbs but no phone. Zoe licked her fingers, doing her best to look guiltless. "Allison is crying happy tears, and she has a s'prise for you on Christmas, and she's gonna bring the phone here in just a minute."

"Don't move!" Sara took her policeman stance. "Hands in the air!" She ran to the bathroom and grabbed a damp washcloth. When she returned, James stood in the doorway.

"Are they being arrested?"

"Yes. They're cookie thieves." The girls giggled as Sara wiped mouths and fingers and blew at the crumbs on two pink shirts. Brushing would smear the chocolate. She took longer than she needed to and realized it made her look like exactly what James had so often called her—a clean freak. In reality she was far less concerned with Oreo bits than with the scent of Corduroy aftershave wafting her way from the man in the navy blue shirt and leather jacket. Her eyes—and hands—simply needed a hiding place.

"Do they need to make restitution?"

Sara looked up into eyes that glinted like moonbeams on Lake Superior. "I think we'll give them a pass this time. They kept a few carbs out of Allison's mouth."

"Mmm." The moonlight left James's eyes. "You ladies ready?"

Trying to read the sudden shift in his expression was futile. For some reason just the mention of Allison's name had set him on edge. "Have to get boots and jackets and hats and mittens. . .and probably make a potty stop. Other than that, we're ready."

The sparkle came back, turned on like a light switch. James let out a long, exaggerated sigh. "Women. . .so high maintenance." He winked at her. "Put me to work."

"Jackets are on the hook behind the door and—" A giggle floated through the open doorway. James stepped into the room and turned around.

Allison, wearing a skintight maroon maternity sweater and with her hair actually clean and brushed, held the phone out to Sara. James stared at Allison then reached behind the door for the jackets. Taking both girls' hands, he led them to the couch. The tension in the room was almost palpable. Sara narrowed her eyes at Allison. "You're looking cheery today. What's up?"

"It's Christmas, and I'm having a baby in two months!"

"The last I heard, Christmas was lame and you were sick of feeling like a cow."

"Yeah, well. . ." Allison smiled smugly. "Things change, you know? Gotta split." She turned, not too gracefully, and lumbered back to her apartment.

Sara closed the door. "She's acting weird."

"Yeah." James's voice sounded muffled. Sara turned to see him nuzzling Sadie's ear.

God, if You're listening, please make this work. My girls need their daddy. The prayer wasn't premeditated. It felt strange yet natural. The thought that followed it startled her. *And what do I need?*

That wasn't a question she dared to answer.

❧

Speakers mounted above the chamber of commerce building, the confectionery shop, and the Ben Franklin dime store flooded Main Street with Bing Crosby's rendition of "White Christmas." Tiny white lights lit up store windows and two-foot-wide silver stars glittered from every street lamp. Zoe stood on the sidewalk holding Sara's hand, eyes wide with wonder. "It's sparkly!"

James unbuckled Sadie's car seat and set her on the sidewalk next to Sara. Sadie's eyes looked like giant blue cat's-eye marbles. "So pretty. Princessy pretty."

"How come it's not prince pretty?" James picked her up and brushed his lips across her warm cheek.

Sadie giggled. Zoe answered, "Princes don't like sparkly

things. They like swords and horses and stuff." She stared up at him then tilted her head to the side. "Mommy says every princess doesn't hafta have a prince. Is that true?"

James stared at Sara, who immediately opened her purse and rummaged through its contents, probably looking for something that didn't exist. So his absence had altered fairy tales. He took a deep breath. "Well. . .it's true that some princesses don't have a prince. But I think that God made most princes to want a princess, and they're very, very sad without one."

Appearing contemplative and more like fourteen than four, Zoe nodded then glanced at Sara. "I think Mommy's wrong."

If only we can convince her of that. He watched Sara close her purse then lock eyes with his in a look of chagrin. He winked at her, and the tiniest of smiles tilted her lips. Had his legs buckled like licorice whips when they'd first met? Apparently "weak kneed" wasn't just an expression. She'd curled her hair and put on more makeup than he'd seen her wear yet. For him. Beneath the faded denim jacket, she wore a high-neck sweater that matched her eyes. He was in trouble here. Over his head in love with his own wife.

Setting Sadie down, he took her hand then reached out for Sara's. Linked like paper dolls, the four of them crossed the street to the Ben Franklin store. Before opening the door, he said, "The first present on our list is a jacket for Mommy."

"I don't need a—"

He stopped her protest with two fingertips to her mouth. Her lips were warm. His head was fuzzy. "Do it for me. If you get sick, I'll end up doing laundry and dishes." He grinned at her but cringed inside. He was leaping over her boundaries. The drawbridge could rise and slam shut at any moment.

Sara's face twisted into an adorable combination of stubborn pout and shimmery-eyed surprise. "I have a better idea," she said. "Let's buy Daddy a new jacket, and I'll take his." She fingered the flap that covered the zipper on his jacket.

"This one is too small for you now."

That must be the reason he wasn't able to expand his lungs. She wanted his jacket? The one she used to use as a pillow when they went for picnics on the bluff? The one she said smelled like him and gave her good dreams?

"White Christmas" ended, and Tony Bennett crooned "Winter Wonderland." James looked to his left then his right. He squeezed Sadie's hand then let go. "Did you know, girls, that Mommy knows how to swing dance?" Laughing at the look of terror on Sara's face, he grabbed her other hand, pulled her several feet away, then swung her in a circle. As he drew her close again, her look of fear morphed into a smile.

And then she laughed. Clear and root beer–sweet in the cold, crisp air as Tony Bennett sang, ". . .to face unafraid the plans that we've made. . . ."

❧

Sadie clutched her very own shopping bag as James carried her to the car. Sara, walking behind them with a tired four-year-old leaning against her, waved at her youngest and snapped a picture with the disposable camera James insisted she buy. Sadie gave a halfhearted wave and rested her head on James's shoulder.

It had been a day of scrapbookable moments. She didn't know when she'd laughed so much. Actually she did know. In the first twelve months of their marriage. Twirling on the sidewalk, holding onto James's hands had brought it all rushing back. In the first year, in spite of the growing clumsiness of her pregnancy and then an infant to care for while working two jobs, she'd felt strangely carefree. . .and madly in love. Memories came back more as feelings than pictures, leaving her light-headed and sad. Over the past two years she'd blotted out the good. It was so much easier to focus on the bad. Today had reminded her of what had been and what could be.

But the fun part of the day was almost at an end. Not only

did she dread the counseling session, but at some point she'd have to talk to James about her new job and hope he didn't see it as a threat.

They rode in tired silence to the Lewis Ranch, as Brock and James referred to it. Both girls were sleeping when they got there. Sara carried Sadie, and James picked up Zoe. They laid them on their own beds in their own room, and Sara tried hard not to care that her daughters would wake up with happy squeals in a princess room in a cluttered house with a ten-foot Christmas tree surrounded by a moat of presents they didn't need. Tomorrow night Grandma Connie would dress them in their ridiculous dresses, and there would be too much food and too much wrapping paper strewed about. . . and Sara wouldn't be there to watch her girls have more fun than they'd had in months. She wouldn't be there, but so far she was the only one who knew that.

When they got to the car, James opened the door for her. She slid in and looked up at him as he leaned over the open door, haloed by the garage light. He reached down and lifted her chin with his index finger. "They'll be fine."

Tears stung her eyes. "I know." Just before he closed the door, she whispered, "That's the problem."

She didn't think he'd heard, but after starting Connie's car and backing down the gravel drive, he stopped and stared at her. "This is hard for you."

Not a question but a statement of fact. He got it. Sara nodded. "I hate that I resent her." She forced a swallow. "I never had a chance with her, did I? I can't ever do anything right in her eyes. She shows me up in everything." She bit down on the inside of her bottom lip. It was the only way to stop the flow of words once the lid was off.

James backed the car onto the road. The headlights arced across snow-covered ditches and a barren cornfield. "If I say she means well, it sounds like I'm sticking up for her, but I'm not. It's just that whatever phase she happens to be going through and whatever wacko philosophy she's embracing at the moment is ultimate truth in her eyes. She's convinced it's her calling to enlighten the world to feng shui or iridology or high colonics or raising emus...."

Sara had no choice but to laugh. *Crazy Connie.* "She's... eccentric." Once again it was the nicest thing she could think of.

"She's a nutcase, Sara!" He said it with so much force that she had no idea if she should laugh or stay silent. The set of his mouth told her there was more to come. "She has no clue how many people she's hurt."

This wasn't the first time Sara had heard him criticize his mother, but in the past his comments had been sarcastic at best, often vicious. This time it felt more like regret. "How has she hurt you?" Sara could have made a list, but she wanted to hear it from him.

"I told you about the whole 'destiny' thing. I'm serious when I say that I really believed it. I feel so stupid. When God started opening my eyes to what a wretch I was, it made me sick."

Wretch? Isn't that right out of "Amazing Grace"? Did Christians actually use that word? "That's a little strong." Did she really just say that? "Wretch" was tame compared to the names she'd hung on him.

James smiled. "I'm guessing you used worse on me."

Was he in her head? "I did. Much worse. But it's hard to hear you saying things like that about yourself. You've changed." The one thing she knew he'd been waiting to hear—and it had slipped out like butter in July.

A car passed, outlining James's face, showing the smile her admission had birthed. "My mother's a product of a bizarre family; you know that. How can I blame her for not knowing how to be a mom? She was raised by a stoner and a sitar-playing gypsy! I had to make myself look at all that when I started trying to forgive her for raising me without any discipline or direction."

"You're disciplined in your music. Your mom encouraged

you in that." Defending Connie was foreign territory.

James laughed. "She couldn't have kept me away from it. Music comes under the category of obsession not discipline." He glanced at her. "I don't have to tell you that, do I?"

No. But she wasn't in the mood to say it out loud. In fact, she wasn't in the mood for much of anything other than staring at her husband's profile in the red glow of the dashboard lights. . .or walking hand in hand by the river. . . .

The last thing she was in the mood for was spending the next two hours digging up pain.

sixteen

"What consumes your thoughts, James?" Eldon offered him a second snickerdoodle from a mounded plate.

James shook his head. The cookies were heavenly, but he barely had enough saliva to swallow the first one. "Maybe later." If the night ended on a good note and the inside of his mouth no longer felt like a dirt road.

"Other than Sara and the girls, what's important to you?"

He didn't need to think about that one. "God and music. I try to keep it in that order."

Eldon grinned. "Appreciate your honesty. Can you elaborate?"

"Sure. For a long time my thoughts about the Lord were mostly worship. I'm still in shock that He came after me. It's all still new, and my head's kind of spinning with learning something about Him every day." He ran his hand through his hair, needing something to do with his jitters. "I think I'm in the housecleaning stage my buddies warned me about. I went through all the remorse, looking at what a mess I'd made of my life, and then once I finally got it—that I'd really been forgiven—there was sort of a honeymoon period."

"Kind of a weightless feeling, isn't it?"

"Yeah, that's a perfect description. But lately God's been making me deal with some stuff that isn't so easy." James was only too aware of Sara's every move. As he talked, she tugged at the bottom of her sweater then folded and unfolded her hands, yet her eyes seemed fastened on him. *Lord, let me say what You want me to say.* "Attitudes, mostly, and thoughts. I've been really convicted of how stuck on myself I've been."

" 'Be transformed by the renewing of your mind,' " Eldon quoted.

Mattie nodded. "He's refining you. It gets painful at times."

"I'm not really liking this part, but I wouldn't turn back for anything."

❧

Though she sat just a few feet from the flames that blazed in the Jennets' fireplace, Sara pulled a throw blanket from the arm of the couch and covered her legs. No one else seemed to feel the cold. In fact, they all seemed warm and cozy, eating cookies and chatting like old friends. Mattie sat with her feet propped on the coffee table, sipping her chamomile tea and smiling at James. Sara felt so distant she could have been standing outside the window, chilled by the wind, staring in at the Christmas tree heavy with homemade ornaments, the six stockings that hung from the mantel, and the three people who shared a language she didn't speak. It wasn't that she didn't understand the words. It was that she'd never experienced the emotions that went with them.

Eldon asked James to talk about his "love of music." Sara pulled the blanket to her elbows.

"I feel guilty sometimes that I get paid for playing. I'd sure like to get paid more, of course." The Jennets laughed along with James. Sara made herself smile. "Music is pretty much like food to me. It feels like a basic need."

Bessie's words reverberated in Sara's mind. *"You're afraid of it—the music that pulses through his veins, the thing he needs to feel alive."* Even now, just talking about it, James's demeanor became more animated. Was she really afraid of it, or was she—

"Sara, how does it make you feel to hear James talk about his music with such intensity?"

The question jarred her, pulling her from her isolated place outside the window. She'd vowed to be as honest and transparent as she could. "It makes me sad." She scanned James's face. He nodded, apparently not surprised. "The truth is, I've always been jealous of his music."

Mattie took the pen from Eldon and scrawled something on

the notebook. "Because of the time it took away from you?"

"That and. . .he talks about the songs he writes like they were. . .lovers." Her face burned, but she was determined to press on with the truth. "I wish. . .I used to wish. . .that I could stir as much passion in him as his music."

James looked away. His body language changed. "Rigid" was the word that came to Sara's mind. Her words hung in the air for several too-long moments before Eldon pointed his pen at James. "That's not sitting well with you, is it?"

Silence. The fire crackled. James brought his hands down on both knees then crossed his legs. The *whish* of denim brushing denim amplified in the strained stillness. "It's not sitting well because it's not true. It's true that music took up more of my. . .more of me than Sara. But it didn't have to be that way. If she—"

Holding his hand up just like Sara did with her girls, Eldon stopped James. "Talk to Sara. Remember the rules, and tell her how you feel."

Bitterness scalded Sara's throat. *This should be interesting.* There was no way James could follow the rules—use only "I" rather than "you" messages, avoid "always" and "never," stick to the topic at hand, and don't bring up old disagreements unless they pertain. She stared at the Americana colors in the braided rug beneath the coffee table and waited. James shifted, and she sensed his eyes on her. With a shaky breath, she faced him and waited.

"I. . .wanted you to be the center of my universe, Sara. There was a window of time when I would have given it all up for you."

"A very small window. I guess I missed it altogether."

Her biting tone made James cringe visibly. His fingers curled into his palms. "Think back. Just a couple days before you told me you were pregnant. We were riding bicycles up on the bluffs, and we stopped for a picnic. Remember it?"

Sara's necklace was too tight, forcing pressure into her

head. She'd shoved that day far back in the archives. Cool air scented with leaf smoke, the leaves turning colors along the river. Their lunch was fresh bread, apples, and cheese. They pretended they were overlooking the Seine or the Thames. A perfect day. It was only later that she realized it was all a lie. "Yes." It was more of a hiss than a word.

"Do you remember what I said?"

"Of course." The tension in her face made it hard to talk. "You said you wanted me to go to Canada with you, but if I didn't want to go, you'd stay right here with me." Darts shooting from her eyes didn't feel like a metaphor. "And four days later, you left."

"Whoa!" In one swift motion, James swiveled on the couch to face her. "If you're going to tell that part of the story, tell the whole thing, Sara. Tell about the day you called and told me you were pregnant." His glare pinned her to the back of the couch. "The day I came over to ask you to marry me."

"What?" Time had warped the story in James's mind. There had been no proposal. "You did not."

"Oh yes, I did. I walked into your kitchen, and you were on the phone in the living room, talking to your friend Kim."

Sara sucked in air, but it wasn't enough. She needed to get outside. He'd heard that conversation and never told her? Heard it just days after pledging to leave everything behind for her. Heard it and walked away for three months. What had she said that night? She remembered crying hysterically, pacing the living room, yelling about her life falling apart, her plans shattered. Tears blurred her vision as she forced herself to stare at James.

His eyes smoldered. "You said, 'And now I'm pregnant by a guy I'm not even sure I'm in love with.'"

⁂

Their dance in front of the dime store seemed a lifetime ago. James stared at the blotchy red face of the woman who shared the couch with him as if she were a stranger. His arms no longer ached to hold her, nothing in him wanted to draw her close and stop the sobs that shook her. He simply waited, cold and emotionless, for her to respond.

Maybe this whole counseling idea was a mistake. Was it really necessary to dredge up the ugliness of their past? Couldn't they have just made a fresh start? An unexpected picture dropped into his consciousness—the wall beneath the single window in his tiny London apartment. The landlord had painted just before James moved in. Painted right over the damp, bulging plaster where water leaked in every time it rained. In the two years James had lived there, the paint had peeled and the wet, moldy plaster had crumbled, little by little, onto the floor.

Lord, be my strength.

Sara took a long shuddering breath. "I was scared. I questioned everything. But the moment I knew you were gone"—glittering, pain-filled eyes pleaded for understanding—"I knew. I knew absolutely that I loved you and I wanted to spend the rest of my life with you. But. . ." She wiped her face with a wet tissue, and Mattie got up and handed her a new one. "But then it was too late to tell you that I'd move to Canada—or anywhere—with you."

She'd never told him that. Never. How could two people live under the same roof and leave so much unsaid? That one sentence could have changed the course of their marriage. A silent groan vibrated his chest like an oncoming train. Arms that had felt leaden just moments before crushed Sara to him. Only vaguely aware that they were not alone, he kissed the top of her head over and over.

The Jennets gave them a respectable time, then Eldon quietly asked, "What made you come back, James?"

Swiping at his damp eyelashes, James looked over the top of Sara's head and pressed his lips together in a straight-lined smile. "Life just seemed flat without her." Sara convulsed with a muffled sob, and he held her tighter. "I decided I was going to make her love me if it killed me." *Just like I'm doing right now.*

"What was her reaction when you returned?"

James laughed. Sara reared her head and glared at him, making him laugh even harder. "She was spitting tacks. Slashed me up one side and down the other then fell into my arms sobbing. Kind of like this." He pushed wet strands off her face. "And then I asked her to marry me, and she said yes. My mother was irate, of course, so we ran off and got married in a quaint little chapel in Stillwater, and we had a tough but wonderful first year."

Sara pulled away slowly, as if she hated to leave his arms but needed her space for safety. "It was a good year," she whispered.

Mattie cleared her throat. She seemed in danger of adding her own tears to the mix. "We may want to get back to that first year, but tell us when things started to break down."

"Our first anniversary." James looked to Sara for confirmation, and she nodded. "I get the insensitive-oaf award for that one."

Sara's smile came quick and natural, and James breathed a pent-up sigh.

Sara cleared her throat. "James announced over candlelight and spaghetti that he'd taken a job with a band that was leaving in two days for a three-month tour."

A lopsided grimace twisted Eldon's mouth. "Not the brightest move."

James shrugged. "Now you tell me." He took Sara's hand and squeezed it. "It wasn't quite as awful as she makes it sound. I hadn't officially accepted the job, and I would have been gone for nine days at a time then home for five. I was already working two jobs and not seeing Sara and the baby. The band had a following, and the money would have been double what I was making. And the five days I'd be home, I'd actually get time with my family." He looked from Eldon to

Sara. She appeared almost startled, as if something he'd just said surprised her.

"You didn't take the job?"

"No." James clenched the hand that wasn't holding Sara's.

"Did you talk it over?" Mattie aimed the question at him first then Sara. "Did you discuss possible compromises?"

He could have laughed at that one, but his mood had shifted drastically in the past few minutes. He simply shook his head.

The leather jacket that now belonged to Sara was wedged between her and the arm of the couch. She picked up one sleeve and ran her hand along the leather as if she were petting a kitten. "That was my fault." The same surprised look creased her forehead. "I. . .didn't. . .see it that way." Her hands shook. "All I could see was that you wanted to leave again. I didn't see anything good coming out of it." She looked at Mattie. "It was the first time I ever screamed at him. Not the last."

"She changed. . . ." James remembered the rules and squeezed Sara's hand. "Something changed in you after that."

Sara nodded, brushing away tears. "I knew you wanted to leave. It was just a matter of time, so I had to start thinking like a single mom. I had to be ready."

Sap bubbled on a pine log in the fireplace, filling the room with a quiet, high-pitched whine. The log snapped apart; red sparks shot up the chimney. Mattie pushed the box of tissues across the coffee table. "How did she change toward you, James?"

Shoulders shaking, Sara raised her stop-sign hand. "I became a. . .dictator." Her voice was ragged. "I made him turn in every receipt and keep track of every penny he spent. I'd always made to-do lists for myself, but after that, I made lists for James, too. I made sure there was no time in his schedule for his music. I yelled at him if he played too rough with the girls and yelled more if he didn't spend enough time with them. I told him what books to read them and. . ." She stopped, covered her eyes with one hand. "It was like I needed everything in neat little boxes."

Mattie's maternal smile poured grace on Sara. "You felt threatened, and you needed to control whatever you could."

Eyes wide, like Zoe staring at the lights on Main Street, Sara slowly nodded. "Even decorating was a way of controlling my environment. *My* colors, *my* fabrics to decorate *my* townhouse. It was just another way of making neat little boxes." She took a ragged breath. "I felt driven. . .to create a safe place for the girls. I thought I was just being a good mom, being prepared for what I was sure would happen. . . and in the process I made it happen."

James felt his throat tighten. She pulled her hand out of his and stared into him. The green eyes that had captured him and pulled him back every time he left looked suddenly rainwashed, unveiled. "I made your life miserable, didn't I?"

seventeen

James guided the steering wheel with one hand. Sara encased his right hand in both of hers. Her face felt tight from salty tear tracks as she nestled against the back of the seat, enveloped in a worn brown jacket. Heater vents shot warm air, but for once Sara wasn't cold. She looked over at James. "I have to call my mom and admit she was right."

"About what?"

"She said I clipped your wings."

James laughed. "I don't need wings. I'm not going anywhere."

"But you need to flap around a *little* bit. I didn't give you any room to flap."

Again he laughed. "You're cute."

"That's what I did to God, too, isn't it? I mean, nobody can stop God from being God, but maybe I didn't let Him be God for *me*. Does that make sense? I couldn't see how He could want anything to do with me, so I didn't allow room for Him."

"Everybody's got their own way of resisting. I ran from Him the same way I ran from you, Sara Bear."

Fresh tears threatened. Like a wobbly top, she hovered between crying and laughing. Sara Bear. That was a name she thought she'd never hear again. "I'm sorry."

James's laugh was a soft exhale through his nose. "That's number eight hundred and forty-six tonight." He extricated his hand and ran the backs of his gloved fingers across her cheek. "I'll say it one more time—it's not all your fault. I wasn't the husband and father I should have been. I was immature and looking for excuses to run. Both times. Can we agree, at least for this moment, that we've forgiven each other?"

134

She reached up, turned his hand, and kissed his palm. Once then again. "Okay."

"And you do understand, don't you"—his voice had a breathless edge—"that Jesus is just standing here waiting for you to surrender it all to Him?"

Surrender. This time she was ready to hear it.

James stretched his arm across her shoulders, and they rode the rest of the way in silence. Sara filled the minutes with unspoken words.

Dear God, I'm not holding back anymore. I don't want to hide from You or fight anymore. . . .

❧

James stopped the Escape in front of her apartment and reached for her hand. "I want to pray with you."

Mesmerized by the softness of his voice, Sara could only nod.

"Lord God, You alone have brought us to the beginning of healing. Thank You for loving us in spite of our selfishness. We're imperfect people who will make mistakes in the future, but You know our hearts. You know we want our family to be together and our marriage to be strong. Please save us from our own foolishness and guide every step we make together. Amen."

"Amen."

Reaching above her, he opened the mirror on the visor, triggering the vanity light. "I need to see you," he whispered. In the soft glow, Sara stared back, drinking in every angle of his face, the hair that curled over the collar of his new ski jacket, the creases that framed his mouth. The tenderness in his eyes tampered with the cadence of her pulse.

James pulled off his gloves then slowly removed hers. Warm fingers traced a path from her ear to her chin and followed the outline of her mouth. He leaned toward her until she could feel his breath on her ear. "I love you, Sara."

His words were almost buried beneath the hammering of her heart. Sara raised her hand and did something she'd visualized since the day he'd helped her paint. She slipped her fingers through dark brown waves and let them trail to the back of his neck. "I love you, too."

Feathery kisses covered her face, brushed across her lips and lingered there. He kissed her then in a way he'd never kissed her before, in a way that made her feel not only desired but cherished, protected, and sheltered. His mouth hovered just millimeters from hers. "It's kind of cold out here."

Her eyes were closed, but she heard the smile in his voice. She smiled back. "I'm plenty warm."

"There aren't any children inside."

"There aren't any children out here." She rubbed her nose against his. "Besides, there are rules."

"Whose rules?"

"Sanctuary rules say I can't have any man in my apartment."

James laughed, leaned across her, and opened her door then kissed her again. It was a clumsy kiss, made awkward by his grin. "I'm not any man, sweetheart. I'm your husband."

༄

Laughing like teenagers, they ran up the snow-dusted sidewalk. James opened the door, scooped her in his arms, and carried her into the foyer while Sara fished in her purse for her keys.

"What's that?" James pointed at a square of yellow paper taped to her door.

"Probably a phone message. Allison's my social secretary." She laughed and nibbled his ear. With a mock groan, James dipped her toward the door so she could stick the key in the lock and turn the handle. As the door opened, she ripped the paper off the door and read it.

Sara—

Some guy named Reece called for you. Isn't he the cute guy you were kissing?

Al

Feeling her face become warm, she stuffed the note in her jacket pocket.

"Anything important?"

"No."

"Good." James closed the door with his foot and carried her to the couch, sitting down with her on his lap. "Have I told you lately that I love you?"

"That's a Rod Stewart song. You can do better than that, Lewis."

"You're right. I can. Have I told you lately how grateful I am that we have another chance to make something beautiful out of us and that I want to take care of you for the rest of our lives and be the best dad I can possibly be and help you manage the Stillwater Inn and make it a huge success and—"

"Shhh. . ." She held up her hand.

He wove his fingers into hers. "You don't believe me?"

Sara shook her head. "We need to talk about the Inn. It's my dream not yours."

"But if it makes you happy. . ."

"What will make me happy is when we find some way for us both to do what we love. I don't want you to give up your music."

James closed his eyes, just for a moment, as if stemming tears. "Thank you."

"We don't have to figure that out right now."

"Are there more important things we should be concentrating on right now?"

"I. . .think so. . ."

He touched the tip of her nose. "Like what?"

The glint in his eyes unraveled her last shred of reserve. "Like this." Sliding off his lap, she stood and held out her hand to him.

&

Sara cracked four eggs and beat them with a wire whisk to the rhythm of the tune that had circled in her head since her eyes opened and she'd realized that, this time, James was not a dream.

Have I told you lately. . . Snippets of the lyrics filtered in, and words she'd never before paid attention to slowed her rhythmic beating—*There's a love that's divine. . .we should give thanks and pray to the one. . .* She had no idea if Rod Stewart was referring to God, but that's what the words now meant to her. She remembered Mattie telling her months earlier that God could use anything to get his message across. Apparently even a rock song.

God, thank You for my husband.

As the simple prayer formed in her mind, she poured the eggs into a hot frying pan—and strong arms slid around her waist. "Merry Christmas, beautiful." Mint-scented breath tickled her ear. "You saved an extra toothbrush and razor just in case?"

"I always have extras. You know I'm all about being prepared." Looking down at his bare arms folded tightly across her holly-leaf apron, she laughed. They could be posing for the cover of *Recipe for a Godly Wife*. Maybe she'd curl up with the book with the bent spine and wrinkled pages after James left for London.

If she hadn't been held tight against him, she would have doubled over at the thought of his leaving. They hadn't talked about that yet. He had a job waiting in London.

Turning in his arms, she laid her face against his chest. James reached behind her and shut off the burner.

ɚ

As soon as he started making some money, he'd buy her a new bathrobe. Something green and warm that flattered her figure better than the shapeless orangey-pink thing that had probably been donated to the Sanctuary program when some ninety-year-old nursing home resident died.

James stared across the table as he chewed slowly on a piece of bacon that was done to perfection. "This is delicious." He hadn't had bacon done right in two years. And he hadn't had breakfast with a woman in just as long. That was something he was immensely grateful for. Considering the crowd he'd hung with, it was nothing short of God's miraculous intervention.

"It's nice to have a man to cook for." Sara topped off his coffee.

He took a careful sip from the murky green Pine Bluff Community State Bank mug. "I'm buying you new dishes with my first paycheck."

"You? Shop?"

"Me? Shop? Not a chance. Me *pay*."

"I thought you'd changed."

"I have. All the bad stuff is gone. The good stuff stayed."

"Mattie says we need to compromise."

James made a show of squirming in his seat. "Uh. . .yeah. . . okay, so if I give in and endanger my reputation as a man's man and start shopping, what would you do?"

"Eat a hot dog."

He'd picked the wrong moment to take another sip of coffee. Tiny brown spots spewed from his mouth and spattered the housecoat. He grabbed a napkin, first for his face, then, sliding to his knees in front of her, he dabbed at her robe. "You are *not* getting by that easily."

She ran the fingers of both hands through his hair, sending shivers along his arms. "Fine. Name something."

"Go to church with me tonight." James held his breath.

"That's all?"

"I thought you'd have a problem with that."

Her nose wrinkled. "You think you're the only person God can change? I mean, don't expect me to start quoting Bible verses or anything, but I'll go to church with you. What else?"

What else? Church was huge, but he wasn't above taking advantage of the situation. "Take me to the airport on Monday and don't cry."

He hadn't factored in Sara's instant tears. It was his turn to hold up his hand in a gesture that once annoyed him. "I have to go back and get out of my lease and give away some stuff and sell some things and give notice on the job I'm not going to take." He'd tell her about the new job once he knew more about it. He used the belt on the tacky robe to dry her tears. "And then pick me up again on Saturday."

&

Connie's hairless cat screeched from its wobbly perch on a high bough of the ten-foot Christmas tree. Sadie, in her rainbow dress with a purple crown on her head and a yellow plastic canteen filled with cranberry punch around her neck, clambered onto an end table and reached out to the cat. Her stocking feet slipped, juice splattered onto the pile of coats on the floor, and Sara screamed. Grandpa Neil grabbed the cat with one hand and caught Sadie just as her face grazed a sequin- and pearl-covered Styrofoam ball. Over Sadie's cries and Grandpa Neil's deep laugh, Granny Charity thundered on the piano and Connie, sitting beside her, sang "Grandma Got Run Over by a Reindeer."

Sara kicked a path in the wrapping paper and got to Sadie just as James took her from his father. She locked eyes with him and couldn't do anything but laugh.

"I told you you'd be glad you came!" he yelled over the din.

Her protest was drowned by the doorbell chiming out "Jingle Bells." Brock, who happened to be standing in front of it, opened the door, and Allison stepped in. The singing stopped. Connie clapped her hand down on her mother's, halting the music. One by one, every aunt, uncle, and cousin stopped talking, and the room became funeral home quiet.

Brock took Allison's coat, folded it over one arm, and put his arm around her. Smiling like he'd just returned from multiple root canals, he cleared his throat. "Mom, Dad, everyone. . .I've been watching James the past couple weeks and listening to him talk about God and what it means to be a man of integrity, and he finally got to me. Or I don't know. . .maybe it was God who finally got to me. Anyway, I made a decision. . . . Allison and I are getting married. My baby needs his daddy."

A *thud* echoed in the deathly quiet room. Sara turned to see Connie, white slits for eyes, wedged between the wall and the piano bench.

eighteen

Monday morning dawned without a hint of sun. Fitting, James thought, for the mood at the ranch. He rolled over, twisting in the crazy quilt like a worm in a cocoon, wishing he was waking up in a double bed instead of a single. They'd decided not to confuse the girls by having him stay for two nights and then leave for a week. At the moment, it didn't feel like the right decision. But then, not much of anything felt right.

His bedroom beneath the east gable still smelled of charred ham from what should have been Christmas dinner. Yesterday, after coming home from whatever it was she was doing in town on Christmas morning, his mother had labored, with long, loud sighs of martyrdom, over ham and scalloped potatoes then locked herself in her room. James left to spend the day with Sara and the girls, taking Brock with him. When they returned for dinner, the table in the dining room was set with Granny Charity's best dishes. In the middle of the table, next to lit candles in silver holders, two black, brick-looking objects were smoking on china platters with serving forks. His mother stood at the head of the table, pointing a carving knife at Brock and seething, "This is all your fault."

They went out for Chinese.

James tugged his pillow over his face but couldn't block out the smell of blackened potatoes and petrified ham. Still under the pillow, he groped for the lamp switch and then his Bible. *Lord, this is going to be a hard day. I have some tough questions for Brock. Grant me wisdom when I talk to him. And I don't want to say good-bye to Sara, even for a few days. Please give me something to hang on to.*

142

Propping on one elbow, he opened to Psalm 28 and read a passage he'd highlighted in yellow. *The Lord is my strength and my shield; my heart trusts in him, and I am helped. My heart leaps for joy and I will give thanks to him in song.*

Song. They'd missed church on Christmas Eve because of all the drama. Withdrawal symptoms were setting in after three weeks of no communal worship. He got up and pulled on the jeans and sweater he'd worn the day before, scrunching his nose at the burned memories floating up from his clothes.

In the corner of the room, right where he'd left it two years ago, was the ten-year-old Gibson Hummingbird guitar he'd sell to a buddy back in London to pay for his one-way ticket back to Minnesota. And there'd be money left to buy Sara some clothes and dishes. . .and maybe a real wedding ring. He picked it up and sat down on the bed to tune it. He was good—not great—on the guitar. Music didn't seem to flow through his fingers to strings the way it did on ivory. He played a few chords until a tune took shape. A Kutless song—"Strong Tower." As music filled the garret room, he prayed. *You are my strong tower, Jesus. My shelter and my fortress. . .*

He heard the phone ringing and then his mother's footsteps trudging up the stairs. Setting down the guitar, he opened the door to his mother, perpetual tears clouding her eyes. She held out the phone. "It's Reece Landon. Though why you'd want to talk to that man, I can't imagine."

Because "that man" holds the key to my immediate future. James took the phone and then, surprising himself as well as his mother, wrapped her in a quick hug. "It's all going to work out, Mom."

"Right. That's what you said when *you* got married."

❧

The patch of sky Sara could see from her kitchen window looked dark and heavy on Monday morning. Even an hour after turning up the heat, cold air seemed to lurk in the corners. She tiptoed into the girls' room and laid another blanket over them.

As she pulled a second sweatshirt from her dresser drawer, it occurred to her that maybe the feeling of cold was merely the absence of the warmth she'd awakened to on Saturday morning. She slipped the sweatshirt over her head as she walked down the hall.

She'd gotten out of bed earlier than usual to face a to-do list as long as the pencil she wrote it with. Allison was coming over to watch the girls at nine so that she could drive out to meet Reece and tour the cabins his family owned on Whitebark Lake. After that she'd meet James and Brock for lunch. She and James had agreed on some "intervention" questions to find out if Brock was acting out of sheer obligation or genuine love for Allison. After that she'd drive James into the city for his four o'clock flight. . .and do her best not to cry.

She peeked in on the girls again. Sadie's hand rested on Zoe's forehead, but both were sound asleep. Relieved, Sara picked up a clothes basket. She needed to go downstairs to the washing machine and get James's new jacket, hoping the cranberry-juice stains she'd pretreated had vanished. She opened the door to the foyer just as Raquel opened hers.

"You're up early."

"Yeah. I need to talk to you." Raquel hadn't worked on Sunday yet looked as though she'd been up all night.

"Come on in." Disappointment settled on Sara's chest. Raquel appeared to have been drinking.

Raquel sat at the kitchen table, and Sara poured the last of the coffee into a mug and slid it in front of her. She didn't smell alcohol. "What's wrong?"

"Your mother-in-law paid me a little visit yesterday."

"On Christmas Day?"

"Yeah. Merry Christmas." Tears balanced on Raquel's mascara-clumped lashes.

"What did she say?"

"In a nutshell? She said, 'Your daughter's worthless, my son's not going to marry her, and if anyone's gonna raise Brock's child, it's me.'"

Sara slid her chair closer to Raquel and put her arms around her. She desperately wanted to say that she must be exaggerating or there must be some misunderstanding, but she couldn't. "She can't do that, Raquel."

Raquel pulled away. "Oh yeah? Tell me you're not scared to death she's gonna find a way to take your girls. I've heard you say it! You're scared she's gonna have you declared unfit. And look at Allison. She's still in high school, she doesn't have a job, she's living on handouts, and her mother's an alcoholic. What chance does she have against that lunatic woman?"

This wasn't the time to talk about all that had transpired with James in the past week, not the time to mention that she no longer harbored those fears. "It'll be okay. Nobody's going to take that baby."

Raquel wiped her face on her sleeve. "This is what I get, isn't it?"

"What do you mean?"

"My punishment. If I hadn't messed up my life, Allison wouldn't be pregnant and—"

Latching onto Raquel's shoulders, Sara waited until she looked up. "Listen to me, Raquel. I don't know much yet, but I know one thing. Jesus loves you and Allison and that baby, and He's got good plans for all of you. He's just waiting for you to surrender. . . ."

❧

"What do you think?" Reece swept his hand toward the great room. "Just imagine leather couches and rustic tables."

Sara stared at a vast expanse of newly varnished hardwood floors then moved on to granite counters, black kitchen appliances, and a stone fireplace that spanned two stories. This was the second cabin they'd looked at. The first, right next door, had a hot tub in the finished basement.

"When you said 'cabins,' I was thinking *Little House on the Prairie*."

"My family doesn't do small."

"I guess. You're sure that cleaning isn't involved in this job?"

Reece laughed and glanced at his watch. "You're just the scheduler. I'm hoping to hire someone today to manage things here. You'll be answering the phone, checking e-mail, making reservations, and taking credit card info. We'll supply you with a BlackBerry and a laptop and train you on our computer system." He pointed toward the window. Huge drops of icy rain splatted the glass. "Let's get out of here. There's someone I want you to talk to. We'll take the car to the third house; it's a hike. We call this place North Point because. . ."

Sara listened but couldn't concentrate. Her mind was on the leaden sky and the sleet that had the power to ground James's plane and give her one more day with him. Reece held the door open, and she walked out onto a wide front porch. She looked up at the pewter clouds and smiled.

"Watch your st—"

It didn't happen, like people often say, in slow motion. It was instantaneous. One moment she was stepping onto the first step, staring at the ominous sky, a heartbeat later she stared at the same sky from a totally different angle. Her bottom sat on a step, her head on the porch.

"Are you okay?" Reece kneeled beside her, his face distorted by so much concern it made her want to laugh.

"I'm fi—" Little white stars danced in the corners of her field of vision. The back of her head throbbed, and something else hurt. The pain seemed distant; she couldn't quite focus on where it was coming from. "Help me get up."

"Are you sure you should?"

"Yes." She shivered. "We're getting wet."

Reece helped her to a sitting position. At the end of the long, rutted driveway that swayed before her eyes, his yellow

BMW swung like a giant banana on a string. Sara clenched her eyes and fought nausea. The dizziness passed, and she opened her eyes. "I'm okay. Let's go."

"I'm taking you to the hospital." Reece looked at his watch again then toward the car, a good hundred yards on the other side of the frozen ruts that would be a paved drive next spring.

"Just get me up. I have to meet James."

Reece draped her arm across his shoulders and slowly raised her. A gasp ripped from her throat. "My ankle!"

The little white stars came back, and one by one turned black.

☙

James hummed "Strong Tower" as he navigated the narrowing gravel road. The windshield wipers played backup. Glancing down at the directions Reece had dictated over the phone, he wondered if he'd missed something. It was hard to believe there were luxury cabins at the end of this skinny winding path. Thankfully he was a good half hour early. If he had to turn around and hunt down a phone, he could probably still make the meeting on time. It wouldn't do to make a lousy first impression on the other staff members or Reece's dad or whoever he was meeting with this morning.

A crack of thunder shook the car. The wipers swiped a clean view as he rounded a bumpy bend in the road. A blurry streak of yellow took on the form and shape of a BMW. James breathed a sigh and eased on the brake. Another swipe revealed Reece, leaning against the car.

With Sara in his arms.

☙

"James?"

Was that really her voice? She sounded like Sadie, helpless and whiny. Kettledrums banged a solo in Sara's head. Opening her eyes was not an option. "James?"

"It's me. Reece."

Why. . . ? Oh. . .the cabins. . .the ice. . .the rain. It came back to her in chunks. "What time is it?" Would she have time to change before driving James to the airport?

"Five to four."

Sara's eyes shot open then squinted at Reece and against the light. Where was the cabin? The yellow car? Five minutes to four? Panic rose like a flood surge. She tried to sit up, but the room spun. A room with pale blue curtains for walls. "Where am I?"

"The ER. You sprained your ankle, and you've got a mild concussion."

"Is James coming?"

Reece had a strange look on his face that turned up the volume on the kettledrums.

"You called James, right?"

A shoulder shrug and upturned hands were her answer.

"Call him and tell him he can get a later flight, but he has to come and watch the girls and"—a tear rolled from each eye onto the paper-covered pillow—"and tell him I need him to take care of me and tell him—"

"Sara." Reece put his hand over hers. "James doesn't have a phone."

❧

James whizzed past every other vehicle on I-494, picking them off like clay pigeons. *Bing. . . Bing. . .* His mother probably had no idea her Escape could do ninety. At what point would they call out the helicopter to televise his escape in an Escape? The irony made him smile. His hollow, fun-house laugh bounced off the dashboard.

Traffic slowed ahead and forced him down to only seven miles over the speed limit, but his thoughts passed a hundred.

Sara could explain away the hug his mother witnessed as a gesture of friendship, but no one would call what he'd seen two hours ago a friendly hug. Sara had faced away from Reece, her head tipped back on his chest—just the way James had held her in the kitchen on Saturday morning right before. . . He pressed his fingers against his eyes until they hurt, and colored sparks shot like sparklers. But it didn't block out the picture of Sara, eyes closed, face raised to the rain. And Reece's arms, wrapped around his best friend's wife.

He opened his eyes and swerved to avoid the side mirror on a pickup. A whisper of common sense invaded his rage. In the state he was in, he could hurt someone. He got off at the next exit and pulled up to a gas station. A cup of hot coffee might take the edge off and let him think. By the time he turned off the ignition, second thoughts plastered his conscience. He'd just done what he'd vowed not to do. He'd run—again—without getting all the facts. There had to be some explanation. He knew Sara. She loved him. Maybe he hadn't seen what he thought he'd seen. Maybe the rain had distorted his view more than he realized.

He pulled the keys out of the ignition and slipped them into the pocket of the leather jacket. . .Sara's leather jacket. Something stuck to his fingertips. The yellow sticky note Sara had found on her door.

Sara—
  Some guy named Reece called for you. Isn't he the cute guy you were kissing?

James no longer needed coffee. His thoughts no longer chased each other like rabid dogs. He knew exactly what he needed to do. The key slid into the slot, starting the Escape.

Starting the escape. . .back home. . .to England.

❧

Sara opened her eyes in a princess room. Sparkly purple shades restrained the morning. Glow-in-the-dark stars lit the lace-trimmed violet canopy above her. On the bedside table, Cinderella circled the base of a night-light to the tune of "A

Dream Is a Wish Your Heart Makes." Sara groped for the switch. Cinderella wouldn't finish her waltz this time.

Because Sara Lewis didn't believe in dreams.

At first, she'd worried. Lying in the emergency room, her head competing with her ankle for a ten on the Visual Analog Scale, she'd imagined dozens of gruesome reasons why James hadn't met Brock and hadn't gotten to a phone to call him. Reece had intensified her anxiety by explaining that he'd planned a surprise—James was to meet them at the third cabin so that Reece could offer the two of them the job of managing all the cabins on Whitebark Lake. The salary he quoted her while she lay shivering on the gurney was more than Sara had made in her life. It would have solved everything but meant nothing until she knew what happened to James. Was he out there in the sleety rain at the bottom of a ravine? Somewhere on the mud-slick, twisty-turny road to the cabins? Injured? Unconscious? Or worse?

Her panic finally earned her a shot in the hip, which made her less frantic but not less fearful. When Brock showed up in the room with blue-cloth walls, he danced around the truth, but Sara stopped him, just like she did Cinderella, and made him tell her. Made him tell her that James hadn't answered his page at the airport, that James had gotten on the plane, leaving only an eight-word phone call behind: "The keys are under the seat. Sorry, man."

Twenty-four hours later, she was here, surrounded by pixie dust and magic wands, listening to her girls playing hide-and-seek with Connie, smelling homemade corn bread, and feeling like Sleeping Beauty before she awoke. Cold, numb, lifeless.

The drums in her head were muted now, but the muffled beat was relentless. It pounded out a single word. Why? Why? Why? Why had he changed his mind? Christmas Day had been perfect. Too perfect? Is that what scared him? Why hadn't he said good-bye? Even if he'd changed his mind, even if he'd decided they couldn't work it out, why hadn't he said good-bye to the girls?

This time she wouldn't bounce. This time she would follow James's example—as soon as she could walk, she would run.

nineteen

"She had extra toothbrushes and razors in the bathroom. Did I mention that?" James sat on the floor of his two-room apartment and stared at his friends. "She always used to just in case of company, but this time I know it was in case Reece—"

A meaty hand on his shoulder stopped his rant. "We need to pray over James, guys." The burly, bald-headed man with a cockney accent tightened his grip, and the other four members of the accountability group surrounded James. "Lord Jesus, our brother here is in an awful state. He's mightily in need of guidance and a touch from Your merciful hand. Show Yourself real to him and. . ."

James felt rigid muscles yield to the weight of their hands and their words. Blessings and petitions flowed over him like a Mozart concerto. With these rough, life-scarred brothers, he didn't pretend to be strong. When tears spotted his faded jeans, their grip on his arms and shoulders only grew stronger.

In the three days he'd been back in the damp cold of London, he'd leaned on their strength and welcomed their counsel. Tonight, however, their prayers came after an hour of grilling James like a crime suspect beneath an interrogation lamp. They'd questioned his reasons for leaving and challenged him to go back and be the father his children needed, even if he could never be a husband to Sara. Knowing they spoke the truth, he'd fought them with everything in him. He missed his girls with a physical pain that made it hard to breathe, but he didn't possess the kind of strength it would take to go back to Pine Bluff and compete for their attention with the man who had won Sara's.

After the men went home, James flopped back on his thin mattress, staring at the cracks that surrounded the single lightbulb like sun rays. The Tube rattled the bulb, and the rays shimmied. His phone rang, but he didn't get up to answer. Three days' worth of calls filled his voice mail box— mostly from Brock, a few from his mother. Amazingly, even three from Reece. Not one from Sara.

He hadn't listened to a single one.

James tried to pray, but his pleas seemed to go no further than the brittle plaster. From behind a barred door in the shadows of his consciousness, a voice prodded him to listen to the wisdom of his friends. James reached across the bed for his MP3 player. He didn't care what he listened to, as long as it was loud.

The song that blared through his earphones wasn't one he'd downloaded. His country-loving little brother had been messing with his stuff.

Josh Turner sang "Another Try." And James pressed the heels of his hands against his eyes.

"Let her go without a fight. . . . Next time I'll hang on. . .if love ever gives me another try. . . ."

❧

Just one more day.

Sara hobbled through the Lewises' cluttered living room, passing Granny Charity snoring in Neil's recliner. Barbies and Legos scattered out of her way with a swat of a crutch tip.

Voices rippled like rain from the kitchen. She didn't have the strength to witness yet one more example of "every day's a party," but she needed coffee to brighten her voice before making the phone call that could begin her independence.

The sink overflowed with dishes from breakfast and last night's supper, and the kitchen floor was sticky from the applesauce Connie and the girls had cooked days ago. Two hours after lunch and the girls were still in their pajamas. Three days ago, when Brock had brought her home, Connie had taken command. "I'll take care of everything, dear. I don't want you lifting a finger."

But someone needed to.

"Good morning—I mean, afternoon—lazy bum. That was a long nap." Connie drew out the "loooong." Hula hoop earrings banged against her cheeks as she clucked at Sara. "My girls are making *Mother Earth* suet holders for the birdies."

Your girls? Sara glared at the jumble of twisted coat hangers, birdseed, suet, and pinecones that littered the kitchen table. Sidestepping Connie, she kissed Zoe and Sadie on the tops of their heads. "The birdies will be very happy."

"Yook what we got. . .yickyish!" Sadie waved a rope of red licorice under Sara's nose.

"Ewww!" Just the sight of it made her feel pregnant. She looked over at Connie. Surely her mother-in-law knew her quirky relationship with red licorice—that what she craved during pregnancy nauseated her any other time. Was the woman that calculating?

"It's all natural, dear. It's good for them."

"Mm-hmm." Sara backed away from the smell.

Zoe grabbed her sleeve, bed-head curls scampering across her forehead. "Know what? We're going on a long ride to take Granny Charity home today."

Sara lifted an eyebrow and aimed it at Connie. "Oh, really?"

Raising peanut butter and sunflower seed–covered hands, Connie shrugged. "Well, Neil and Brock are working, and I can't leave them with you. We'll start out in an hour or so and be back in the morning, unless the weather gets too bad."

Not on her life.

Sara still had occasional dizzy spells. Her ankle was sore and swollen and throbbed with every beat of her pulse. But it wasn't broken. She could walk if she had to. Sara opened her mouth to argue but was saved from words she might regret when Brock kicked a plastic tiara through the door from the dining room. "I'm off until tomorrow night. Allison and I can watch the girls."

Fire shot from Connie's narrowed eyes, but she didn't say a word.

Brock ignored the fire. "Why don't you wait a couple days, Mom? It's gonna start snowing before dark, and it's not like Granny has to get home for anything."

"I've had enough of her." Connie's voice lowered, and her head dipped toward the living room. "I need to take her home. Today."

Brock's gaze latched onto Sara's, passing a restrained smirk.

Sara returned the look. Clomping back to the counter, she reheated morning coffee in the microwave and stared out the window while she drank it. Shadows lanced the snow-covered yard like javelins. As Sara sipped the Costa Rican coffee that Connie assured her was grown on a small organic farm in volcanic soil, she did something that didn't make sense, even to her. She prayed. *Lord, I know I don't know You very well yet, but I'm trusting You to get me away from here and do what's best for my girls.*

She didn't know where the fragile trust came from. It wasn't simply desperation. As soon as she could manage things at home, Reece would set her up with everything she needed for her new job. She was grateful for that, of course; yet, by her choice, it was only temporary—a bridge to the one dream she still clung to. Maybe, just maybe, God would answer this one prayer and move her farther from her mother-in-law's clutches.

She limped back to the living room. Picking up the phone, she dialed the number she hoped would be hers before long. While it rang, she prayed again.

"Stillwater Inn. *God morgen.* This is Ingrid."

"Hi, Ingrid. This is Sara Lewis."

"S–Sara. How are you, dear?"

"I'm fine." There was no need to tell her the truth. "I just hadn't touched base with you for so long, and I wondered if we could get together and talk. I've been thinking that it would be a good idea for me to work with you. . .um, *for* you. . .for a while before you actually turn things over to me." She rehearsed her next line, how she'd offer to do the books, answer phones, or even bake while she couldn't walk. But it would only be a week or so until she could change beds or clean or whatever they needed. And the single room at the end of the hall would be just fine for her and her girls. Her very quiet, well-behaved girls.

Ingrid Torsten was silent. A squeal of laughter came from Sadie in the kitchen. The room seemed suddenly dark. "Ingrid?"

"Umm. . .Sara. . . We've been meaning to call you. Erik and I have changed our plans. We're going to buy a campground in New Mexico with my brother. So we'll be selling the house outright. Like I said, we were going to call you. . . ."

❧

Brock picked up Allison, and the two arrived less than five minutes after Connie left. Sara imagined them waiting at the crossroad for the Escape to pass. They fixed a snack for the girls then bundled them in snowsuits.

Sara watched from the couch. Shifting the ice pack on her ankle, she propped it once again on a stack of pillows. Just one more day. Her plan was to be home in her apartment tomorrow before Connie got back. Allison had already promised to spend the night on her couch or whatever she needed.

She felt eerily calm and strangely relieved since talking to Ingrid. Her future was no longer a mystery. She would work for Reece. Every day would not be a party. There would be no castle at the end of the path. But she would save, and maybe someday she would buy a house. And she would be all her girls needed.

Brock put on his jacket and sat down next to her. "We're going to hit the hill behind the house before it gets too bad out there. It's snowing pretty hard, and the wind's supposed to pick up."

Sara's eyes burned. Losing her last dream had produced a numb sense of resignation—not tears. But watching Uncle Brock with her girls reduced her to mush. She put her hand on Brock's. "You guys will make good parents."

Brock snorted, his eyes sparking. "James said you were going to try talking me out of marrying Allison."

"I was. You guys are still babies yourselves, you know. I'm worried about you. But seeing how sweet you are with Allison and watching you two with my girls—I don't know—maybe I was wrong."

"It took me awhile to figure out if I could be a decent husband and father."

Sara's eyes closed for the space of a breath. "You just have to. . ." Her voice squeezed to a whisper. "Just be there."

A look of pain twisted Brock's features. He stood then bent and kissed her on the forehead. "Take a pain pill, and go to sleep while it's quiet."

"I will."

Allison walked through the dining room with an armful of hats and mittens.

"Al, will you have a car tomorrow to give us a ride home?"

"Not till four. Mom's working a double shift. I could bring your car. . .if it's not buried in the snow by then."

"That'll work." Sara sat back. She had an escape strategy.

Allison wiped Sadie's nose and tied her hat. Sara motioned for Allison to come closer. Grabbing her hand, she squeezed it. "Thank you."

"It's nothin'. I'm almost their aunt, you know."

"I know." Sara put a hand on Allison's belly. "And I get to be Aunt Sara to this little person. We're going to be sisters, Al."

Self-consciously Allison giggled. "Yeah, we gotta watch each other's backs." She glanced at Brock and whispered, "Gotta protect each other from the wicked witch."

❧

Sara stood in the middle of the Mall of America, staring up. Four stories above her, James leaned over the railing, dangling his leather jacket. "Catch it!" The jacket took flight, soaring like a hawk, and landed at her feet. She put it on. It smelled like James. Looking up, she giggled. "I'm getting dizzy!" she yelled. "Come down."

He reached toward her. "I can't. I can't find Zoe, Sara. Where is she? Is she in here? Is she with you, Sara? Sara. . . Sara. . ." His voice blended with the howling wind and the sound of snow pelting the windows. Four stories of windows. . . so loud and echoing. "Sara! Sara!"

Rough hands shook her.

"James?"

"Sara! Wake up. Is Zoe in here?" It was Brock, standing over her, dripping snow on her face.

Her head felt funny. She was dreaming, just dreaming. The pain pills gave her strange dreams. She closed her eyes, but Brock tapped her cheek with cold hands.

"Sara! You have to wake up. We can't find Zoe. Did she come in here?"

Fear shimmied from the base of her spine. Her eyes snapped open. "What do you mean you can't find her?"

"I mean I can't find her!" His voice rose. He paced, his hands on his head. "We've covered every inch of the yard and the house and looked up and down the street."

"Weren't you watching her?" Sara sat up, grabbing for her crutches.

"She went down on the sled. Allison and Sadie and I were at the top of the hill. Zoe got off, but instead of coming back up, she ran around to the front of the house. I called her, but she didn't come." His words came faster. "I've looked. . . everywhere. She just. . .disappeared."

❧

It was just after twelve when James crawled into bed. He

was almost asleep when the phone rang. That would be Brock. That was his trick, calling every day after supper when he knew it would be midnight in London. The ringing stopped then started up again. "Not a chance, little brother." James pulled the blanket over his head and prayed he'd sleep through his dreams.

It felt like he'd just fallen asleep when a rap on the door woke him. "Mr. Lewis?"

"Who is it?"

"Metropolitan Police, Mr. Lewis. Open up."

James scrambled into jeans, his brain inventing scenarios as he stumbled toward the door. He imagined his car—smashed or missing tires—or one of the guys bleeding from a fight. He opened the door and nodded at the man in the dark blue hat with a silver crest. "What is it?"

"Mr. Lewis, your daughter is missing."

twenty

Afternoon light crept around the corners of the sparkly purple shades. Sara stood in front of the open closet in the darkened room. She'd come in here to get away. Away from Sadie's incessant questions, from her mother calling every half hour, from the ringing phone that brought no answers and a roomful of eyes asking how she was doing. She came in here to keep from screaming. But she couldn't get away. The closet floor was strewed with dress-up clothes. "Zoe. . . Oh, God. . .my baby girl. . .where is she?"

She picked up a pink leotard and a glitter-coated high-heeled shoe and pressed them to her chest. Her lips were dry and cracking, her eyes hot. Her throat ached. And yet there were still more tears. She threw her crutch and folded to the floor.

Mattie walked in and sat beside her, wrapping one arm around Sara. "They've posted the Amber Alert."

Sara pulled one knee to her chest.

"The storm's dying down. The roads will be cleared soon."

Not fully comprehending what that meant, Sara nodded.

Mattie placed a hand on Sara's head. "Lord Jesus," she whispered, "You are all we have. Hope is what we cling to—"

Brock walked in, sat on Sara's other side, and held out the phone. "Honey, James is on the phone."

Sara stared at the phone then looked at Brock. Fresh tears tracked along her chin. She didn't care what he'd done or why he'd left her again. She needed James here. "I. . .okay." She took the phone. Mattie and Brock left. "James?"

"Sara. . ." His voice was rough, gravelly. "I'm in Chicago. We're waiting for the runways to be cleared in Minneapolis.

160

Eldon's going to pick me up. I'll be there soon."

Sobs jarred her. "I. . .I. . .can't. . ."

"I know. I know. Is there anything you can tell me? What are you thinking, Sara? Do you think my mother took her?"

"Ye. . .yes. But where would she leave her? The police picked up your mother at Granny's, and Zoe wasn't with her. She won't tell them, James. She won't admit to anything, not even to your dad. And what if she comes back for Sadie? And what if it wasn't her? There was a guy. . .at the health club. . . . Your mother let him watch the girls and. . .and. . .I should have told her no. What if. . .what if he—"

"We'll find her, honey. And. . .Sara. . . ? I don't care what you've done. We're going to get through this together, okay?"

Sara rocked, still hugging the shoe. "What? What do you mean? What have I done?"

"I saw you, Sara. I saw you with Reece. . .at the cabin."

"*What?*"

"We'll talk about it later. When this is all over."

"No!" Glitter bit into the palm of her hand. "What did you see? Is that why you left?"

"I saw the two of you by the car." His voice caught. "His arms were around you and—"

"I sprained my ankle, James. I had a concussion. I fainted. Reece dragged me to the car and. . .we were waiting for you. He was going to surprise us by offering us the manager job. . . together."

The sound he made was part gasp, part groan. "Sara. . ."

"You didn't stop. You didn't trust me enough to find out the truth?" Her words formed on short, tight breaths. "If you'd been here. . .I wouldn't be at your mother's, and Zoe. . . wouldn't. . .be. . .gone."

❧

An hour and twenty-one minutes to Minneapolis, the pilot announced. Minutes stretched beyond sixty seconds. Time distorted. He leaned his head next to the window, not taking his eyes off the clouds and glimpses of snow-covered land. *Zoe. . .where are you, baby?*

Guilt, regret—the old demons he'd almost defeated—embedded their claws. *Lord, I'm so sorry. I wasn't there for her. Find my little girl. Bring her back safe.*

❧

God, find her. Find her. Bring her back to me. Sara sat on the edge of the couch, staring at the plow on the front of Neil's truck, widening the straight-walled tunnel to the road. The phone rang again, as it had all day. Sara closed her mind to false hope and kept her eyes on the plow. Fourteen inches in less than twenty-four hours, plus drifting and blowing. Drifts licked at the top of the split rail fence and the bottom of the mailbox. Fourteen inches. . .high enough to cover a little girl. Deep enough to—

Allison screamed. Sara whirled around to see her break into tears, clutching the phone.

"She's okay! Sara, she's okay. Zoe's with my mom." She held the phone out.

Sara grabbed the phone and sank onto the couch. "Raquel?"

"Sara. . .I'm so sorry. Zoe's fine. I'm so sorry. I. . .I took her. Just for a little while. . ." Her voice quaked and convulsed with sobs. "I wanted Brock's mother to know what it felt like to lose a grandchild. I was on my way to my sister's. . . just ten minutes away. I was going to call you as soon as we got there. . .I was going to ask you to go along with it to give that woman a good scare. But we went into a ditch, and the car got stuck. I couldn't open the doors, and I didn't have the phone. They're just digging us out now. I called the police when the tow truck got here. I told them everything. I'm not a kidnapper, Sara. I didn't want to hurt you, not you. . . but when Brock's mom came to see me again and said such awful things about keeping Allison's baby and taking us to court and. . .I'm so sorry. It was so stupid. I can't imagine how scared you were. I'm so, so sor—"

"Let me talk to Zoe." She couldn't listen to another word from Raquel.

"Hi, Mommy."

"Baby. . .are you okay?" Dark spots dotted Sara's vision. The room swayed. She closed her eyes and bent over the phone. "Are you okay?"

"We had a sleepover in the car, Mommy. We played games and ate candy, and I got cold, but Raquel had a blanket, and now the police is gonna take me home. Is that okay? He's not a danger, is he?"

"No, baby, he's not a danger. He'll give you a ride and. . . Daddy will be home when you get here."

❧

Bundled in James's new blue jacket and balancing on one crutch, Sara stood shivering on the back step, watching Eldon's car navigate the Lewises' driveway. Before the car came to a complete stop, James jumped out and leaped over the snow bank. Ignoring the shoveled path, he hurtled the fence and ran toward her in knee-deep snow, his gaze locked on hers. His eyes were red and swollen.

"Sara. . ." Several feet in front of her, he stopped. "Sara. . . I'm so sorry. . ."

The sound that came out of her was half laugh, half cry. She held out her free arm. "Just shut up, and give my jacket back."

In a breath, he stood beside her, engulfing her in the familiar smell of leather and Corduroy. He lifted her chin. His lips skimmed her wet cheeks and brushed over her eyes. The sound of tires on hard-packed snow pulled him away. The squad car drove up. Before Sara knew what was happening, James had lifted her off her feet. The crutch fell to the snow, and James carried her down the sidewalk. An officer opened the back door, and Zoe jumped out, blond curls springing from her stocking cap. "Mommy! Daddy!"

Sara slid down, stood on one foot, leaning on James's arm

while he scooped Zoe up in the other.

Zoe put one arm around James's neck and one around Sara's. "Why are you crying?"

Burying her face in Zoe's hair, Sara sobbed. "Because we missed you, sweetie." Pink mittens stroked her wet cheeks, making her cry even harder.

"Can we go home now to our real house?"

Sara stared at James. His eyes asked the question she'd answered in her head hours ago. "Yes."

"Do I get to keep my Daddy now, for real?"

James blinked back tears. "If Mommy will have me in spite of my stupidity."

"Mommy, do you want daddy's spidity?'

"Yes. I want Daddy's spidity if he can handle all my silly rules."

"Yay!" Zoe wriggled out of their arms and ran down the path, toward the crowd gathered by the back door. "Sadie!" She waved at her little sister, wrapped in a blanket in Brock's arms. "Sadie! We get to keep our daddy. . .forever and ever and ever!"

ॐ

While James talked with Pastor Owen by the front door, Sara occupied the girls in the foyer of Pineview Community Church. She watched James gesturing with his hands. The music director had just gotten a job transfer, and Pastor Owen wondered if James would be willing to lead the worship team. *Lord, You are so good.*

Raquel came out of the sanctuary, squeezed Sara's arm, and headed for the exit without a word. Her face was streaked with mascara. Good tears, Sara hoped.

For the third time, Zoe held out the picture she'd drawn in Sunday school. For the third time, Sara bent to admire it. "Tell me about it."

"It's Nowhere and the ark. And these are the aminals. . . ."

As Zoe rattled on, a woman approached and stood a few

feet away. When Zoe took a breath, Sara turned and smiled at the woman. "Good morning."

"Hi, Sara. I don't know if you remember me. I'm April Bachelor. I interviewed you. . .twice actually. . .after the Sanctuary fire and after the tornado."

"Oh, I remember you. I've been watching your TV show, but seeing you in person again makes me a little nervous. I kind of associate you with disaster."

April laughed. "I hope I can change that." Honey blond hair skimmed her shoulders as she shook her head. "I just met Raquel. She told me what happened with your daughter. Talk about grace in action."

Sara shrugged. "We understood Raquel's motives." *Only too well.* After they'd gotten over the initial anger, she and James had been in agreement about not pressing charges. Ironically it was still harder for Sara to extend daily grace to Connie than to Raquel. But little by little, she was working on it.

"I was also talking to Mattie Jennet this morning. I'm doing a special Valentine show next week called 'Marriage Miracles.' Mattie says you two have a story you might be willing to share."

Sara pointed over April's shoulder. "Here comes my miracle now."

April turned around and introduced herself to James before Sara had a chance to. She explained the premise of her show. "Would you two be interested in telling your story?"

James rubbed his hand across his jaw. "I don't know. I think our story needs another chapter first." He looked from April to Sara and back to April. "April, I know I just met you, but could I impose on you to watch my girls for about five minutes."

Sara narrowed her eyes. "James. . . ?"

His mysterious smile quickened her pulse. He grabbed her hand and led her down the hall to the music room. Vibrant chunks of gold and blue from the stained glass windows formed mosaic patterns on the dark red carpet. James pulled her into a swirl of sun-born color.

And dropped to his knee.

"Sara Lewis, will you marry me. . .all over again?"

❧

Hundreds of votive candles lit the small stone Stillwater Chapel. Sara stood alone at the back of the church and watched her girls walk hand in hand down the aisle, long white dresses swishing, tiaras ricocheting candlelight. When they got to the front, James reached for their hands and turned the girls to face Sara. The music changed to a piece written by James. . .and played by Bessie. In spite of her pain, Bessie had insisted.

Sara smoothed the front of Mattie's Juliet-style gown, fingering the pink satin ribbon that trimmed the empire waist. Something borrowed. This time, wearing secondhand was an honor.

In black suits, James and Brock waited at the front of the chapel. Mattie, wearing a pale pink dress picked out by Zoe and Sadie, stood on the other side. The small crowd rose to their feet, and Sara walked down the same aisle she had five years ago. She glanced at Connie's profile as she passed her. The look on her mother-in-law's face as she stared straight ahead at her star sapphire son could almost be construed as a smile.

Sara took her place between James and Zoe, and the four of them turned to face Pastor Owen. The music ended, and the pastor prayed then lowered his hands for the congregation to be seated.

"On behalf of James and Sara, I want to welcome you all to this celebration of marriage. Our God is a God of second chances, and this couple. . ."

His encouragement and wisdom surrounded them like sunlight. When he finished, Sara gave her bouquet to Zoe and held her hands out to James. His were shaking, but the look in his eyes told her it wasn't from second thoughts.

Pastor Owen closed his Bible. "And now we have the

privilege of being witnesses to James's and Sara's vows of renewal. James?"

"Sara Lewis, your amazing green eyes stole my heart years ago. And even though I've tried. . .many times. . .to run from them, I'm afraid I'm simply stuck." He waited for ripples of laughter to subside. "I promise, before our Lord and the people gathered here, to put our family before myself, to protect and provide for my girls, and to be there when you need me. I promise to go to marriage counseling every week for the rest of our lives if that's what it takes." He winked at Mattie. "And I promise to be your prince forever and ever and ever." He smiled and whispered, "Zoe made me say that."

James held his hand out to the side, and Brock placed a ring on his palm. James slid it on her finger, next to the plain silver band she'd worn for five years. Two stones in a silver setting. Sara gasped.

"The star sapphire represents the light of Christ. The diamond is for the strength we'll need to finish the race set before us. . .together."

"Thank you." Her mouth formed the words, but no sound came with it.

"Sara?" Pastor Owen nodded to her.

"James, you are the love of my life. I have hurt you in so many ways over the years, and I know it is only by the grace of God we stand here today. I promise to never stop growing in my knowledge of the Lord and never stop learning how to be the woman He made me to be. I promise to read *Recipe for a Godly Wife* over and over until I have it memorized. And from this day forth, I will never again make a honey-do list or tell you how to father your children."

When the laughter faded, Pastor Owen held his hands over them. "Father, please hold this family in the palm of Your hand. Strengthen and protect them, and let Your light shine through them.

"James, you may kiss. . .your girls."

❧

When they reached the back of the chapel, James stopped her by the door. "I got you a little wedding gift." He pressed something into her hand but didn't let her open it. "It's not the castle you've dreamed about, and it won't really be yours for a few years."

Sara's mouth dropped open. She tipped her head to the side and stared into sky blue eyes. The thing in her hand felt sweetly familiar. Her fuzzy pink puff ball. . .with a key attached. Her tears were instant. "Does it come with a grand piano?"

James nodded. "And with a live-in assistant who's been miserable in Arizona."

"That will be"—she wiped her tears with the back of her hand—"a huge help. Because I have a little. . .a very little. . .gift for you, too." She held her bouquet in front of him. From the center of the flowers, she pulled a single red-licorice rope and took a bite.

Creases formed between James's brows. "You hate lic— unless you're. . ."

"Unless *we're*"—she placed his hand just below the pink ribbon—"having a baby."

TIPPET HOUSE HEARTHSIDE HOT CHOCOLATE

(Thick and rich—makes a great dessert all by itself)

5 tablespoons Dutch-process cocoa powder
4 tablespoons sugar
2 cups whole milk
2 cups half-and-half
6 ounces dark chocolate (at least 70 percent cacao solids),
    finely chopped
1 teaspoon vanilla
Freshly whipped cream

In a small saucepan over low heat, combine cocoa powder, sugar, and ½ cup of the milk. Heat until sugar melts and no lumps remain, stirring well. Bring to a low boil, stirring constantly. Add remaining milk and half-and-half. Heat but do not boil. Turn off heat, add chopped chocolate, stirring until smooth. Stir in vanilla. Pour into serving cups. Top with *lots* of freshly whipped cream. Makes 4 servings.

Bessie's Shortbread Cookies

1 cup butter, softened
½ cup sugar
¼ teaspoon vanilla
2¼ cups all-purpose flour
⅛ teaspoon salt

Beat butter at medium speed until creamy; gradually add sugar, beating well. Stir in vanilla. Combine flour and salt; gradually add to butter mixture, beating at low speed until blended. Roll dough to ½-inch thickness on a lightly floured surface. Cut with 2½-inch round cutter or Christmas cookie cutter. Place 2 inches apart on an ungreased baking sheet. Bake at 275 degrees for 50 minutes or until bottoms begin to brown. Cool 2 minutes on baking sheet; remove to wire rack. Enjoy by a fire if possible.

A Letter To Our Readers

Dear Reader:
In order that we might better contribute to your reading enjoyment, we would appreciate your taking a few minutes to respond to the following questions. We welcome your comments and read each form and letter we receive. When completed, please return to the following:

Fiction Editor
Heartsong Presents
PO Box 719
Uhrichsville, Ohio 44683

1. Did you enjoy reading *Stillwater Promise* by Becky Melby and Cathy Wienke?
   ❏ Very much! I would like to see more books by this author!
   ❏ Moderately. I would have enjoyed it more if

   _____

   _____

   _____

2. Are you a member of **Heartsong Presents**? ❏ Yes ❏ No
   If no, where did you purchase this book? _____

   _____

3. How would you rate, on a scale from 1 (poor) to 5 (superior), the cover design? _____

4. On a scale from 1 (poor) to 10 (superior), please rate the following elements.

   _____ Heroine   _____ Plot
   _____ Hero   _____ Inspirational theme
   _____ Setting   _____ Secondary characters

5. These characters were special because? _____

_____

_____

6. How has this book inspired your life? _____

_____

_____

7. What settings would you like to see covered in future
   Heartsong Presents books? _____

_____

_____

8. What are some inspirational themes you would like to see
   treated in future books? _____

_____

_____

9. Would you be interested in reading other **Heartsong
   Presents** titles? ❏ Yes ❏ No

10. Please check your age range:

    ❏ Under 18   ❏ 18-24

    ❏ 25-34   ❏ 35-45

    ❏ 46-55   ❏ Over 55

Name _____

Occupation _____

Address _____

City, State, Zip _____

Cranberry
HEARTS

$\mathcal{T}$hree women's lives have
been turned upside down,
but will life's changes
and dangers lead to love
in and around Boston,
Massachusetts?

Contemporary, paperback, 352 pages, 5³/₁₆" x 8"

Presents

Great Inspirational Romance at a Great Price!

Heartsong Presents books are inspirational romances in
contemporary and historical settings, designed to give you an
enjoyable, spirit-lifting reading experience. You can choose
wonderfully written titles from some of today's best authors like
Wanda E. Brunstetter, Mary Connealy, Susan Page Davis,
Cathy Marie Hake, Joyce Livingston, and many others.

When ordering quantities less than twelve, above titles are $2.97 each.
Not all titles may be available at time of order.

HEARTSONG
PRESENTS

If you love Christian romance...

$10.99

You'll love Heartsong Presents'
inspiring and faith-filled romances by
today's very best Christian authors...Wanda E. Brunstetter,
Mary Connealy, Susan Page Davis, Cathy Marie Hake, and
Joyce Livingston, to mention a few!

When you join Heartsong Presents, you'll enjoy four
brand-new, mass-market, 176-page books—two contemporary
and two historical—that will build you up in your faith when
you discover God's role in every relationship you read about!

Imagine...four new romances every
four weeks—with men and women like you
who long to meet the one God has chosen as
the love of their lives...all for the low price
of $10.99 postpaid.

Mass Market 176 Pages

To join, simply visit www.heartsong
presents.com or complete the coupon
below and mail it to the address provided.

- -

YES! Sign me up for Heartsong!

NEW MEMBERSHIPS WILL BE SHIPPED IMMEDIATELY!
Send no money now. We'll bill you only $10.99
postpaid with your first shipment of four books. Or for
faster action, call 1-740-922-7280.

NAME_____

ADDRESS_____

CITY_____ STATE _____ ZIP _____

MAIL TO: HEARTSONG PRESENTS, P.O. Box 721, Uhrichsville, Ohio 44683
or sign up at WWW.HEARTSONGPRESENTS.COM